COMPKILL

She sat in his bedroom, dry-eyed but terrified. She was virtually kidnapped. Her body, to be used again and again by him, was its own ransom! What in God's name had she gotten into?

She listened at the bedroom door, hoping that somehow she'd be able to make a break for it, when the door buzzer rang. She heard him let somebody in. Muffled voices.

... "Run a program to verify the corrections have been made and then order a wipe on this ... what's his name?"

"Smith. John Smith."

"Christ. All right—order a wipe on this Smith. That goddamn diode hit more systems than I thought. I hope this is the last of it."

A wipe. She knew they were talking about murder.

ATTENTION: SCHOOLS AND CORPORATIONS

PINNACLE Books are available at quantity discounts with bulk purchases for educational, business or special promotional use. For further details, please write to: SPECIAL SALES MANAGER, Pinnacle Books, Inc., 1430 Broadway, New York, NY 10018.

WRITE FOR OUR FREE CATALOG

If there is a Pinnacle Book you want—and you cannot find it locally—it is available from us simply by sending the title and price plus 75¢ to cover mailing and handling costs to:

> Pinnacle Books, Inc.
> Reader Service Department
> 1430 Broadway
> New York, NY 10018

Please allow 6 weeks for delivery.

_____Check here if you want to receive our catalog regularly.

Compkill
Gary Paulsen

A TOM DOHERTY ASSOCIATES BOOK
Distributed by Pinnacle Books, New York

This is a work of fiction. All the characters and events portrayed in this book are fictional, and any resemblance to real people or incidents is purely coincidental.

Lines from "Leda and the Swan" are reprinted by permission of MacMillan Publishing Co., Inc., from *Collected Poems* of W. B. Yeats. Copyright 1928 by MacMillan Publishing Co., Inc., renewed 1965 by Georgie Yeats. Permission of M. B. Yeats, Anne Yeats, and MacMillan London Ltd.

COMPKILL

Copyright © 1981 by Gary Paulsen

All rights reserved, including the right to reproduce this book or portions thereof in any form.

A Tor Book

First printing: October 1981

ISBN: 0-523-48016-4

Cover illustration by Paul Stinson

Printed in the United States of America

Distributed by Pinnacle Books, 1430 Broadway, New York, NY 10018

Compkill

PROLOGUE

Sweepkill; diode breakdown without error rectification

In the north there are distances which pale other distances on the planet into insignificance. Hundreds of miles exist between neighbors. It's still possible in the far reaches of the Canadian and Alaskan tundra, for example, to find a thousand miles between a man and his civilization.

The Sweeps. Immense reaches of white and bluish gray that are always cold and always dangerously forbidding in that curious way that seems to lure a certain few men rather than repel them. North Hudson's Bay, the Northwest Passage, sucking men to glory and death in ships and on sledges; killing the Hamiltons and Frobishers, driving those it did not kill with the cold, mad with the desire to return.

Cold, Sweeps, wild winds and white-blue snow—and oil. Buried black treasure of such worth that had those earlier explorers known of it they would have expended their great, greedy energies going down and not across this thankless land. But the amount of oil under the tundras had long defied measurement; the land's fittest challenge yet is for mere survival. Caribou, seals, hares, ptarmigan, bear and small foxes have adapted. And so too—but so rarely as to be striking—has an occasional modern man.

The man standing next to his dog sled with a small, obscure object in hand was one of these. His name was Dale Youngblood. He was white, of medium build and weight, but far from average in other respects. He was of the north, the son of a trapper and his mail-order bride, with a childhood of dogs and wolves and solitary living behind him. Twice Youngblood had tried to leave the north. It hadn't worked. Then, knowing he could not leave any more than a bewitched fool could leave a beautiful woman who was destroying him, he'd tried to lull himself with the sensible gadgets technology had introduced to the north. But they hadn't worked for him either. While others he knew ran snowmobiles and set up plastic tents with gas heaters, he'd gone back to the old, hard ways—pushing heavy freighter sleds, bivouacking in oil-heated snow huts of his own making, trapping with snares and deadfalls instead of steel-and-spring contraptions that could shatter at seventy below.

For all his virtues and his faults, Youngblood had been hired by an oil company to traverse the Sweeps and bury small electronic sensors here and there. He was on the job now. The sensors were to measure the approximate size of the oil pools beneath the ice. Since each weighed only four pounds, he could carry a hundred and forty of them on his freight sledge. When he'd finished planting all the devices, their individual signals would be fed into a computer far to the south. There corporate men would listen, observe—and begin to shape up the machinery to exploit the oil so discovered. In the end, these men would ruin the north, Youngblood knew. But he covered up the one sensor and trekked on. It was not a matter he dwelled on. He did not honestly think of much, except where he would stop to sleep and how a cup of sugared tea would taste after he had tied and fed his nine-dog team and chewed on some jerky for a time.

He was three hundred and seventy-five miles north of tree line and on the move. Then, at the top of a ridge, he stopped. Not for himself but for his dogs. They were beginning to pant and spit blood from tongues they'd cut on their harness buckles when they ran. It was during this interval of quiet, while he was tending to the lead dog, that he first heard the sound.

Didn't hear it, exactly, but felt it. A low throb that seemed to come from the ice itself. The dogs heard it as well and peered around, quivering. They could not locate its source. The sound was everywhere around and below and above them and they whined in fear and looked back at Youngblood, something they seldom did unless on command.

He took off his snow goggles, pushed back his parka hood and frowned attentively. The throbbing was slightly louder now, but he still could not locate its origin.

Except that gradually he realized what it was and knew it to be a threat. It had to be a threat, because in this land all unexpected arrivals were threats. The sound was being made by an approaching still-unseen chopper, which had no business coming his way. He felt the danger in his blood even before he did his reasoning.

Youngblood knew he and his team could not avoid being sighted. He grunted and with a heave, turned the sledge on its side to immobilize it. The dogs might still drag it, but only with great effort. Then he grabbed his Winchester from its scabbard on the sledge and made for a nearby ice outcropping. The rifle, as always, was loaded, full in clip and with one bullet in the chamber. He hunkered into a cubby of ice and waited on the sound, which was getting louder all the time in the cold air.

At length the helicopter hove into view from the south, flying low even for a chopper. By then Youngblood had done more thinking, almost too much more. In his loneliness, he was thinking that perhaps he'd been wrong; perhaps it was bringing added supplies or more sensors. He almost stood to welcome it, but at the last moment held back. Something in the intent way the chopper followed his team's tracks across the ice, and in the frightened manner of the dogs, made him hesitate and move the safety of the rifle to fire.

It was very nearly the last action of his life. The helicopter stayed tight to the tracks. When it came up the small ridge where the sledge was turned on its side the right-hand door slid to the rear, the barrel of an automatic rifle emerged and the sledge and dogs were torn by a sustained burst of fire.

Blood and bits of dogs splattered across the snow. Those animals not hit screamed and tore at the traces. Youngblood in his shielding cubby of ice swore, ducked low, then raised back up and aimed the rifle at the pilot's side of the helicopter.

He worked the bolt swiftly. The .30-'06 bucked three times as he sent three one-hundred-and-eighty-grain expanding-core bullets through the thin plastic on the chopper and into the center of the pilot's chest. There was no answering scream, just the nerve-jerk of the pilot's lifeless body. The helicopter immediately spun into the ground as the pilot's hands and feet yanked the stick to the side and jammed the pedals.

There was a white geyser of gas as the tanks ruptured and the engine heat exploded them, then the strange feeling of warmth in the air for the brief time the chopper took to burn.

Youngblood did not take time to stand and wonder at this strange, killing turn of events. There was new danger now, not from the helicopter, but from the Sweeps. He went to the team while the copter was still burning and used the '06 to finish off those dogs badly wounded in the rifle fire but not killed. Four dogs were unhurt, though it would take half a day to settle them down. Four dogs to pull him the hundreds of miles he had to go to reach any real safety. Because one thing was almost for sure; the curtailment of the chopper's radio signals figured to alert the people who had sent it. He had to get going—underteamed or not.

Youngblood did not ponder long on the fact that the helicopter had had the oil company emblem on its side. He would do his pondering—and maybe his reacting—later, after he got back to his base camp. If he got back.

The man didn't know that no amount of pondering could possibly help him understand why the chopper had come on its killing mission. Who was there to tell him that the whole incident had been triggered by the failure of an NCR-21 diode element in the power supply of a computer terminal in Los Angeles, California? That the attack of the chopper was just one minor consequence of a technical breakdown in that terminal—that, indeed, there were far more significant consequences than this one?

Another symptom of NCR-21 failure was occuring in a computer terminal in a farming bank in Shoshone, Colorado, for example. In a little prairie bank.

An error light was flashing in the accounts section.

One

Interface breakdown

John Smith, at thirty-one, was one of those men who often look either younger or older than their age. His eyes were blue, leaning to gray, with expressive corners, and his mouth was straight across. When he was tired his eyes sagged and he looked fifty; when he was feeling up he went back down to twenty-four or five. His hair was short and blond and he had the kind of perpetually slim, strong build that many people with weight problems envied. Which, considering the sedentary nature of his job, was thought extraordinary.

John worked as a computer technician for a contractor in Denver, Colorado, and spent much of his work-time drinking coffee and looking at schematics or logic breakdown diagrams. Often he would sit studying for hours, moving only slightly. But those who knew him at all—nobody was close to him—and were struck by his physical condition, did not know that he also spent much time hunting in the mountains for elk with an antique Sharps Creedmore .50-90 buffalo gun and that it was lugging this medium cannon around that kept his muscles from softening.

There was much else that John Smith's co-workers didn't know about him. He usually worked alone and on those infrequent occasions where he was with somebody he kept conversation to a minimum, almost totally absorbed by the computer issues confronting him. He was, like many computer people, completely caught up in the expression of logic as it appeared in computer usage: channeled logic, logic based on stored memory and put to a specific use. Computer usage fascinated him, even turned him into a philosopher. In his repair and maintenance work, he had access to enough of the codes of different computers to give him almost limitless use of their faculties. He did not talk much because he did not need to talk much; working a quick code program through almost any computer terminal in the world could tell him, he felt, anything he needed to know about anything.

It was perhaps John's proneness to quiet contemplation that had led to the winding down of his own marriage. She had been pretty and open and blonde. He'd been fired up by her gaiety. Unfortunately, it turned out, they'd married too soon, not knowing that when they'd settled down she'd want to keep constantly on the go and he'd want mostly to sit and think.

Now and then, long after their amicable divorce and her remarriage, John Smith thought of her. He was smiling and thinking of her now, mostly of her spectacular legs, when the buzzer in the data control center—John's troubleshooting office—broke into his pleasurable musings.

"Smith," the PA system requested, "come up on line fourteen to the outside."

John sighed and went to the wall phone to punch the specified button. Based in this digital equipment-packed room, he'd often be called out to the various sites serviced by it. He worked on bank and store computers all over eastern Colorado. When one broke down, the main computer business office in downtown Denver would be called and the call would be transferred to him. John wondered what was up. Something interesting, he hoped.

The complainant spoke rapidly. "Hello. This is the cashier at the Shoshone First State Bank. We have an error indication...."

"What number are you?" John took the phone over to the data center's main console, which mounted many switches, a television screen and a typewriter keyboard on its three sides.

"1479 is our identification number, but I'm not sure where the error is coming from. I mean it seems to be coming from outside somehow, like a command error working through...."

"Just a minute." John punched in the ID number of the bank and watched the screen. The cashier, a woman, had a faintly whining sort of voice that irritated John. He tried to remember what she looked like, then realized he probably had never seen her—the Shoshone bank was way out in the sticks and he didn't get out there unless something at the site broke down, which it usually didn't.

"I have you now," John said. "Hold on while I scan."

He watched the screen as he worked in the parameters to make a general scan of the data coming from and going to the bank.

Nothing amiss appeared.

"I don't see any error indication here," he said, sighing. "Would you double check your terminal?"

"I'm looking at it now. The light is flashing."

"Maybe it's the light. You could be having low voltage, causing it to flicker. That wouldn't be serious. Could you have someone there check it out?" It was eighty or ninety miles out to Shoshone and it was a hot July day; he didn't want to drive out there just to fix a goddamn light.

"I'm sorry." The cashier's voice indicated that she wasn't sorry at all. "But I can't run a bank like this with a possible error working in our account computer."

"Terminal," John corrected idly. Most banks didn't have computers; no small ones did. "The computer is here in Denver. That's just a terminal you have, for sending and receiving data. And like I said, I seriously doubt that there is any error other than temporary low voltage or a faulty bulb."

"I could have said that myself." The cashier's voice was definitely snappish now. "I don't feel that we should be expected to operate in this way. Especially when you consider the amount of money we pay you to lease your computer."

Part of it, John thought—you only use a tiny part of the whole thing. The rest is leased by other banks and stores and and and.... "I'll look into it on this end and get back to you, all right?"

"Of course it's all right." Frost—cold. "But I want that light to quit flashing or I want somebody to repair it—I think that's only fair." She was openly angry when she signed off.

John, swearing to himself, went through another scan of the Shoshone operation. Again the scan showed no error. The readout on the television screen was normal in all respects.

He took a sip of coffee from his stainless steel thermos cup. The coffee, by noonday, had become tepid and bitter, but he hardly noticed —the Shoshone problem, as he thought about it, began to absorb him. Say it wasn't the light, but something else. But what? Computer systems and data center equipment were very reliable these days. The days when systems had been immense, with vacuum tubes and huge tape decks, had passed; then a mere change in temperature could erase whole sections of data storage, producing all sorts of hard-to-trace errors. But with solid-state miniaturization and improvements in memory storage systems, computers today were almost stunning in their efficiency. Of course mistakes cropped up, but they were usually made by the operators who fed in the input data and not by the systems themselves. And when something untoward did happen, it was invariably monitored by the equipment and wasn't often puzzling.

John once more envisioned that hot, boring drive out to the prairie. He didn't really want to make it, no way.

He scanned again.

Nothing.

He swore without a great deal of passion and peered at the screen, hoping for an answer that would save him the Shoshone trip the next morning.

TWO

Control

The man studied the girl shrewdly, almost dispassionately, despite the fact that she was standing nude before him, her sensuous young breasts and pubic area flattered by the soft sidelights in his hotel suite. He was a middle-aged man; she expected more from him, at the very least a gleam in his eye.

"Do you like what you see?" she asked tentatively. Even in her uncertainty, her voice had a practiced, lecherous quality. She was an extremely high-priced prostitute and enamored of her career. She loved its accoutrements and paraphernalia—the *sotto voce* input from her answering service to her tape recorder, the clandestine meetings arranged by phone, the financial payoff. All of it excited her so much that she quite often had orgasms while screwing clients. This fact had gotten around and had eventually permitted her to limit her practice to the *crème de la crème*—richly established judges, lawyers, doctors and so on. Never had she wandered from this coterie.

Until now. A supreme court justice friend from another state had recommended that she take on this one man, that he qualified as being handsome and dignified and rich enough for her needs.

He was all of that and more. This man had a silent aspect of power that actually put a hot little worm in her stomach. His eyes were fixed upon her and already she was wet.

He did not say whether he liked what he saw or not. He said nothing, only smiled slightly.

Eyeing him, she sipped the white wine he had asked her to drink while naked. It was a tangy chablis, from Australia or some such place. Just the unfamiliar label on the bottle made her woozy with anticipation. "Is there anything else special I can do for you?"

He nodded. "Dance." His voice was even, modulated only by the huskiness that came from the beginning of sexual excitement.

She shrugged. "That's easy. Is there music?" She raised her arms and ran her hands up through rich, long black hair, piled it on her head and let it fall in a cascade. "Music would make the dancing better."

"What kind?"

"Your choice. Something slow, maybe. With a beat." She flexed her hips. "I'll make it work for you—just for you."

He moved to the wall near the fireplace and punched at buttons on a control panel, then sat back down again in front of her. Quadraphonic sound poured into the center of the room with a suddenness and a quality that made her gasp. It was mostly low-register saxophones and snare drums, so smoothly textured, sensual and supportive that after a moment or two her legs seemed to lift of their own accord.

She moved in small circles, never going more than two or three feet from where he sat, within that perimeter framing her every movement to arouse lust. The tips of her firm, uptilted breasts passed inches away from his mouth as she bent her hips achingly towards him. When she thrust herself upright again, it was to run her long slender fingers down her stomach to the brown-haired juncture of her thighs. The music was almost unbearably sweet. Her lips parted and she licked their corners with her tongue.

He still said nothing, didn't move. But it was obvious to her now that she was exciting him. She moved closer yet and rubbed her groin teasingly against his shirt. She was breathing hard, a fixed if vacant smile on her face, and her eyes were glazed.

"Now?" she said. "Are you ready now?" She reached down to his pants and felt his hard penis. "You feel like it, don't you. . . ."

He grunted, took a handful of her hair and pulled her down on the couch with him. He took her, almost that fast. There was no talk, no foreplay; she had hardly slid under him before he was in her, thrusting and driving relentlessly, his hand clamped over her mouth to still the cries of pain and mounting ecstasy that kept escaping from her. He was smothering her with his power. She wanted him to go on and on. "Now, now, now!" she chortled. "Now you're fucking me—now!" But for all that, for all the surge of joy in her, she did not come. She was not in control, as she most often was with her johns; it was he who was in control. He gave a lurch and a shudder and it was over for him; she was left gasping.

"You...," she began chaotically, "I mean, that...was something. I've never...that was something."

Abruptly, he was on his feet again, his clothes rearranged, a drink in his hand, the same faint smile on his lips.

"Get dressed," he said. "Leave."

She nodded, got to her feet—a bit unsteadily—and found her clothes. "Judge Waring was right," she said as she dressed. "You're nice. Very nice. In a strange way."

"You talk too much."

She tried to find a critical tone in his voice but there was none. Just the same even tone and the smile.

"You should dance more often and talk less," he said speculatively.

She tried answering the smile. "Thank you for the compliment. I think."

He nodded slightly. "I will pay you now." He took a sheaf of bills from his pocket and peeled off a thousand dollars.

"But that's all right," she said, swallowing as she saw the amount. "I'm not like the others. You can pay me later, by mail."

He put the money in her hand. "You will be here next Thursday," he said coolly.

"But that's my day for...I can't. I'm already booked."

He sighed as if bored and put another thousand dollars in her hand.

"But...."

He hit her then, a tight little blow that caught her in the middle of her stomach. Doubled over in pain, she clutched her gut and stared wide-eyed in fear and doubt at him. A tear ran down her cheek; she couldn't believe he had struck her.

He said evenly, "I don't argue with whores. Be here."

"I'm not a who-"

He moved as if to alert her to his point with another blow, but was interrupted by the ring of the phone on the night stand. She stood momentarily transfixed as he spun away and went to answer it. She heard his voice, irritated by another issue, as if he'd forgotten all about her.

"The error wasn't corrected? Why not?" A pause. "Never mind that. Get it done. Now. There won't be any damage done. Find out all the ramifications of the error and report back to me."

He replaced the phone and frowned briefly before turning back to her. The smile had been restored to his face. It was as if he had no sense of continuity as to his actions, as if it had dropped out of his mind that he had hit her. She knew it hadn't.

"Out now," he said tonelessly. "Until next Thursday."

She ran then, on numbed legs, still clutching the two thousand dollars worth of large bills in her hand. She would be back on Thursday, she knew. It wasn't so much the money, because no amount of money, she argued with herself, was worth getting hit for. And she had plenty of money—enough, she thought with a fleeting sense of grandeur, to buy a car a week. No. She knew she would be back because *he* knew she would be back. He had foreordained it.

THREE

Interface breakdown II

Above all else, Richard Landry thought of himself as a businessman. Not a wheeler-dealer or a hustler. A businessman.

He even dressed the conservative part. Gray suits, white shirts and dark solid ties were, he liked to think, his bulwark of conservatism in an age moving too licentiously towards sweaters and jeans. Besides, he was past forty and had a small paunch, and his suit jackets could be fitted to hide it. Otherwise, Landry was quite proud of his appearance; despite a bit of a drinking problem, he had clear eyes in a square, handsome face and was as tall and broad-shouldered as any of the Green Bay Packer football players he admired. He could carry the ball. Let no one get in his way. He discarded disgruntled employees like used-up jockstraps.

The business Landry was in was located in Milwaukee, publishing books for children. His company was small but on the face of it had access to a profitable share of the bookstore market. But that was only on the face of it. Landry was habitually in the red. He couldn't keep a competent editor or secretary anymore than he could a wife. He'd had four of the latter. He went through financial resources as fast as he did friends, functioning always on the edge of bankruptcy and on the edge of his nerves. His life was a pattern of intricate lies constantly on the verge of catching up with him.

"Mr. Landry?"

Landry, not looking from his desk, growled at his current secretary, a young lady in her third day who had already decided to quit. "What is it?"

"There is a man to see you. A lawyer."

"What's he want?" Landry snapped.

"I don't know."

Landry's head shot up. "Didn't you ask him?"

"No."

"Jesus Christ, what the hell's the matter with you, shit head?"

She kept her voice down. "You *couldn't* pay me enough." She turned and walked out of the office.

Landry, hearing her collect her belongings outside, shrugged. There were always more where she came from; there were broads who couldn't get enough of the glamour of publishing. He waited until she slammed the door on the premises, then stood and went out to the reception area. A studious young man was gazing at a wall photo of one of the company's book jackets. He was holding a Gucci attache case and had the air of a wealthy ignoramus.

"Can I help you?" the publisher said suspiciously.

"I don't know. Are you Mr. Landry?"

"Why?"

"I have something to tell Mr. Landry. It's

rather personal. About his business."

Landry studied the young man's neat attire and decided to take a chance on his not being one of those fancy-dressing process servers. "Come in. I'm Landry."

The man nodded. "Allen Chambers of Dodds, Keys and Parsons. My card." He followed Landry into his office and sat easily in a chair the publisher tended to reserve for important authors—which was any aspiring talent whose cheaply bought work might help keep the company from insolvency for a while. Landry rather hoped the young man was one such.

"Now, what is it you want?" he asked pleasantly enough.

"Nothing. I've got it all."

"What is that supposed to mean?"

"You're done, Landry. That's all. You're out of business. I'm here to take over the company on a temporary basis, until the new manager comes in."

"Just what the hell are you talking about?" Landry's neck became red. "Get out of here before I call the law."

"But I am the law. You apparently merged some time back with a company owned by one of my firm's clients. At that time you signed certain contractual obligations. . ."

"What company was that?" Landry said irritably.

"Wisconsin Enterprises. Forgive me. I should have told you straight off."

"But that was a 50-50 merger. I needed. . . ."

"Money. You needed money and W.E. provided it. It saved your company, then." The young lawyer smiled. "However, you agreed, for that money, to observe Wisconsin Enterprises' stipulations as to growth procedures, in short to change some of your management policies. You didn't. I'm stepping in to take over. Of course you will receive whatever payment is still due you. But your administrative responsibilities have ceased. For confirmation, I advise you to phone your attorney. He has already been apprised of W.E.'s intentions."

Landry stared at him. Then he grabbed the phone, punched the button that automatically rang his lawyer's number and learned from his secretary that he was out to lunch. He slammed the phone down. "Shit."

"A thoroughly understandable comment. I can easily understand your feelings." The young lawyer stood and moved to the door. "I will be taking a look at the rest of the office if you need me."

"The hell you will."

The lawyer shrugged. "If you wish, I can get a court order in a half hour, along with a marshall to remove you."

"You can't. It would take days."

"Believe me—we can. Now. I will take my look around while you try your lawyer again to verify all I've said." He moved off. Landry felt rage rise in him. He tore at the phone again, and tracked his attorney to Phillipe's, a fashionable restaurant and watering hole he should have known Murray would be imbibing at. Swearing, he had him paged at Phillipe's, then, when the phone was taken to his table, raised his voice in a bellow. "Murray-what-the-hell-is-going-on-I'm-losing-my-business-you-son-of-a-bitch!"

"Yes, Richard. I know it."

"You *know* it."

"I suggested when you insisted on that merger that you couldn't live up to its terms and would lose your ass. You didn't listen. So now it has happened. I don't know how they caught up with you, but they did. There's not a damn thing I can do about it. Listen, Richard, I've got a client waiting so if there's no further talking we need to do about this...."

Landry slammed the phone down, his face still white with anger. Then a slow, tired flush spread over his features. He looked blankly at all the executive aids on his desk, in particular, for some curious reason, at the magnetic paper clip that held other, smaller paper clips in a long, winding trail. He could not seem to get the parts of his life together. Nothing hung right for him. He tried to think seriously for a moment. He thought about the funds he had "legitimately" held back from his salesmen and authors on the basis of computer printouts he had taken great, conscientious care in forging. He tried to think the word "legitimately" to himself in a way that he could believe, but he was unable to—it kept coming up with quotation marks around it. He thought of his other, even weightier embezzlements. What his thoughts came down to was that he would do time. W.E. would step in and expose him. He would actually go to prison. There was no way around it. He was going to go to jail. For a long time. He would be an old, totally wasted man when he got out.

Slowly, in an act of smooth deliberation, Landry put his cigarette out and went to the window. It was nine floors down. Not much but enough. He took his executive chair and rammed it through the floor-to-ceiling windows. He was careful to break out all the corner shards, fully aware that the dropping glass alone was attracting a crowd of downtown shoppers below. Then as if stepping onto a stage, he stepped out the window. A few seconds later, the body of Richard Landry merged intimately with the sidewalk in front of a well-dressed woman shopper from Appleton. The splattered lady screamed and fainted dead away.

All of it, the arrival of lawyer Allen Chambers, the suicide of Richard Landry and the screaming woman, was but another consequence of the failed NCR-21 diode.

FOUR

Interface breakdown III

Thirty miles outside of Denver, John Smith began to feel glad he'd made the trip. The prairie was in full July heat, to be sure, but in full July bloom as well. In the sweltering city smog it was easy to forget that wheat stood green-gold out here, and that even the short prairie pasture grass, grazed down by beef cattle, had a sweet-smelling green tightness to it that did wonders for the soul.

He had his Sharps gun with him. He'd go on out to Shoshone, fix the lamp in the computer terminal, then find a back road home through the prairie and enjoy himself. Maybe he would run into a stand of ground-squirrels or jump some coyotes—either demanded almost impossible long-range shooting with the old rifle, and he was eager for the challenge.

In the meantime the morning drive was dispelling what little depression he felt over having to come out and work on the bank terminal. By rights, he could have sent a subordinate technician on this job, but there was something about this whole incident that made him want to wind it up himself. For one thing, the cashier's whining complaint had gotten to him. He wanted to make certain that nothing could be left for her to complain about—she was the kind of squeaky wheel that needed grease to keep his job running smoothly.

The road east deteriorated rapidly. By the time he'd gone through Elizabeth and Kiowa the blacktop was a series of holes and cuts from weather and frost heave during the wild winter storms of February. He slowed the truck, but still made good time across the wide flats, and when he came upon Shoshone he was surprised at the suddenness of it.

The town nestled in a fertile basin in the prairie. This was cattle country. The ample pastures attracted large ranches, nine or ten thousand acres on the average, and the beef on the hoof moved a lot of money through the Shoshone bank.

John drove in across Shoshone Creek and found the bank on the edge of a cool plaza shaded by tall cottonwood trees. The plaza and the bank too had an old-style western feel to them. Everything was soft and dapple-green outside. Inside, the bank had raw wood walls with the brands of local ranches burned in them, and there were rustic western paintings hung in the entry hall back down towards the office. They were real western paintings, all right, of horses being broken and roundup scenes with cowboys in chaps holding ropes—all of it in a studied primitive style. The bank's ranch atmosphere completely belied the fact that it was run by computers, that, indeed, such a small bank couldn't be run without computers in the competitive modern market.

John, with the off-hand feeling that he was parading through a bunkhouse, walked past the tellers' cages and through a rear door to the accounting offices. Here was a different bank, filled with cable-runs and the hum of sophisticated equipment. Four decidedly non-rustic workers were busy at the machines.

"I'm Smith," he announced to the group. "I'm here about the terminal."

One of the men looked up. "Oh. You'll want to see Carol. Just a minute, I'll buzz her." He did so. "Carol the complainer?" John couldn't resist commenting while waiting. The man shrugged, grinning. "She's not half-bad. You'll see."

In a moment Carol came out, and John swallowed his surprise. She was a harried looking young woman, to be sure, but she was a smashingly attractive one—a high-cheekboned brunette in her twenties with bold, vibrant black eyes.

"Oh. Hi," she said with what seemed to John to be affected carelessness. "Why don't you come in my office for a cup of coffee?" She turned and he followed her, still pleasantly astonished at how different she looked from his mental picture of her. She had on a nifty pair of designer blue jeans and he couldn't seem to take his eyes off them until she swung behind her desk and sat facing him.

He took the coffee the girl offered him and sipped it. "I came about the light," he said lamely. "Must say, I'm glad I did."

She nodded. If her voice, with its nasal twang, almost spoiled the enjoyable fantasy he was having about her, what she had to say definitely spoiled it. "I wish you'd called this morning—or I should have called you. The light's all right now. You didn't have to come."

"Oh." He smiled away his disappointment. "Well, it figures. That's how it always seems to go."

The girl hesitated. "Could we buy you a lunch or something?" She meant the bank, obviously; nothing personal in it. "It seems such a waste for you to drive all the way out here for nothing."

"No problem. It's my job." John shrugged. "As long as I'm here I'll just check the system out, make sure your terminal is working smoothly."

"Oh. That's not necessary," she said quickly.

"It's no problem," he repeated. "I'll just take a few minutes."

"Actually, we'd rather you didn't just now. We're really very busy."

He caught something off-kilter in her voice, or thought he did. He didn't know what it was. Fear? No. Something else. Something tight and controlled, something extremely cautious. But why? What was wrong here, so that he couldn't look at the terminal? "I wouldn't be disruptive," he said, watching her face, "and it might save you problems later."

"Still, we'd rather you wait until the regular monthly maintenance check. We are, as I said, very sorry that you've had to make this ride out but as you put it, it's your job." A cold air of finality now, but with that same something hidden in her voice.

"Of course," John said, shrugging. "It's your bank. I'll do as you wish."

"That's how we wish," she said. "And now, if you're done with your coffee. . . ?"

He wasn't, and he noted she'd forgotten her offer of lunch. But he put the cup down, stood and went to the door. "See you next time," he said, and walked out.

For a full minute, John sat in his truck in the parking lot, thinking. He wondered what Carol the cashier had to hide. Or why she would think she had something to hide. It was just possible the bank was up to some illegal shenanigans, maybe moving some funds they didn't want him to learn about. But to have a changeabout come so suddenly—one day Carol bitching about the light and the next telling him to back off—just didn't make sense.

He shrugged and started the truck. Probably he had misread the lady. In all likelihood, the bank *was* very busy with normal transactions—the group in the accounting room had certainly looked it. Besides, it wasn't any of his business. He was still in the country. He had his rifle. He went out of town on a gravel road that led north to do some hunting.

About four miles north of Shoshone he found what he was looking for—a cut-bank ledge full of ground-squirrel holes. He stopped the truck and studied the bank through binoculars. In moments he was completely engrossed in the fine art of varmint shooting, totally removed from banks or cashiers or flashing lights.

Normally coyotes kept the squirrel population down, thus eliminating the need for control killing. But coyotes had been trapped out to protect the area's fast-growing, profitable lamb crop, with the result that the ground-squirrels had multiplied rapidly, bringing with them fleas and the danger of plague. The easiest way to get rid of the fleas was to take out the squirrels.

Varmint shooting. Control shooting of a species. John didn't get too involved in the ethics of it, and in any case he rarely hit a squirrel with his big Creedmore—far less often, say, than did the modern shooters who used powerful scopes and high-velocity small bore rifles. John's Creedmore had iron peep sights originally designed for long-range shooting of buffalo. When shooting ground-squirrels he counted "close" as a hit. He was always close. More to the point, the great, barfing rifle's black powder cartridges made a thunder that echoed for miles. It was utterly satisfying to shoot. The recoil set his shoulder back and the cloud of smoke brought memories of the times the Sharps dominated the prairies—it was like living in history when he shot this rifle.

After a moment he saw what he wanted. One part of the bank was covered with holes and squirrels were moving in all directions, now and then stopping to sit up and look around.

The squirrels were a full hundred yards, perhaps a bit more, and he nodded with satisfaction—a perfect stand.

He brought the Sharps case out of the gun-rack and took the rifle out of the leather tube. It was, as always, heavily oiled, and he used a rag from the glove compartment to wipe the excess from the barrel and stock. There was minor pitting in the steel, but the oil kept it stabilized and the gun wouldn't alter its characteristics in his lifetime.

From the glove compartment he took a case of fifty cartridges, long brass tubes he'd loaded with antique equipment, and bullets he'd cast from an original nineteenth-century mold.

He dropped the lever and inserted one of the cartridges. Then he brought the block back up—it came up very tightly for a gun so old—and looked again to the cut-bank, only this time without binoculars. From now on he would use no modern aids for shooting.

At length he picked a squirrel that, sitting up, appeared as nothing more than a slightly reddish dot against the buff-beige of the gravel bank. He rested the rifle on the hood of the truck, eared back the hammer, raised the rear sight and looked through the aperture across the front bead. The bead covered the whole squirrel plus some of the dirt.

He checked the sight again, verified that it was set for a hundred yards, then looked through the hole once more.

He took a breath, held it a moment, let it out. Then he took another, let half of it out, put the front bead back on the squirrel and squeezed the trigger gently. The double-set lock backed off and tripped the hammer. The prairie morning was torn by the roar of ninety grains of powder pushing four-hundred-and-forty grains of soft lead across one hundred yards of grass and dirt. It was, incredibly, a perfect shot, the best possible one with such a rifle, an absolutely centered hit. The huge, round-nosed slug tore into the squirrel's very middle.

John stood, looking across the hood of the truck at what was a once-in-a-lifetime event for a varmint shooter. He was overcome with perplexity. He felt no thrill. Normally, he would have been overjoyed about bringing wind, load, squeeze and sights together in such a classic shot. Much lesser shots had won tournaments. And yet there was something chewing at him, nibbling away at his enjoyment, something that he did not understand.

Frowning, he put the rifle back in the leather case, tied the end shut and put it back in the gunrack. Meticulously, he closed the cartridge box, which held great significance for him and which he loved—it had once been used by a professional buffalo hunter—and put it back in the glove compartment. He got in the truck, reached for the key, then stopped, not starting the engine. Instead, he poured himself a cup of coffee from his thermos and sat looking across the rolling endlessness of the prairie, pondering on what was bothering him until he figured it out.

Shoshone Bank.

It was like a piece of sand in his eye. He couldn't just let it lie there. Despite his attempt to rationalize Carol the cashier's peremptory dismissal, the incident gnawed at him. Where was the bank's manager, for instance? Why hadn't he been there to greet him? It was his data control system. It had broken down. He was obligated to fix it, to find out which part of it was functioning on an incorrect program.

The malfunctioning of his own system—his inability to enjoy the varmint shooting that usually came natural to him—was like a flashing "error" light keying John in to what he had to do.

FIVE

Systemcheck, phase I

John Smith had long since grown comfortable and easy in the computer world. In the early days he would have been called an egghead, a slide-rule freak, or worse. And he would have been set apart, with his strange little plastic tuning wand and other gear, as a dangerous threat to working-class jobs. And he might have played the part, too. After all, early computer people were indeed a special breed, being mostly trained in the military and at select company schools. Taking on a kind of perverse pride in this, they had actually worked hard at maintaining their elitism. They tended to carry about with them little gizmos that nobody else understood, sometimes as a practical necessity but sometimes not.

But then computers had proliferated and spread into literally all facets of human life. Now there were more people working for or on computers than in any other field. As that began to come about, John had been only too glad to get rid of his badges of distinction. He cleaned out his gadget pockets, threw away his tuning wands—they weren't used anymore anyway, what with superminiature circuitry and plug-in systems—and concentrated on probing the more fundamental uses of logic and storage systems.

It was fascinating work. In the end, that was what kept him involved in data control systems when—if he had his drawling druthers—he would have set up a home on the range and hunted big game for the rest of his life. There was no part of the modern world not dominated by data systems. They ran it all. If you knew the right computer keys, you could unlock any door on the planet.

If you knew the keys.

He had driven back from Shoshone and come straight to the data center, leaving the rifle with the security guard rather than taking time to go home first. Now, settled into his chair at the control room console, he gave his mind over completely to the problem of finding out what was going on at the Shoshone Bank. To prevent any extraneous data from cluttering his thinking, he'd wiped his programs.

His coffee was cold but he took a sip anyway. Then he punched in the code for Shoshone and stared blankly at the screen, which now showed only the code number of the prairie bank.

What kind of mistake wouldn't they want him to know about? That was the core question—the kind of mistake.

A money mistake.

That much he could guess. It was a bank and banks dealt in money; anything hidden they didn't want him to know about most certainly had to do with money. Well, he thought grimly, go big or stay at home. He typed in a command to see the fluid assets of the bank. A general, approximate figure.

Seven point four million dollars.

John was a mite surprised. The sum seemed a bit high for such a small bank. Considering the size of the surrounding ranches and the area economy, however, it was probably right. At least, there was nothing flagrantly wrong about it that they'd want to hide from outsiders' eyes.

He frowned. If it wasn't money...no, it *had* to be money. He erased the figure and punched in the code for account discrepancies, overdrafts and the like. But even as the screen went into a row of numbers, erased, started another row and kept going through all the accounts that had been overdrawn, he knew he was taking the wrong approach. This would show nothing. It would be easy to hide an overdraft or an illegal loan, easy to make the latter *look* legal. Besides, that trick wouldn't make the error light flash.

He stared at the screen without seeing, letting his mind take over. What would make the error light trip?

An error light was like an idiot light in a car—preset to come on and alert the non-knowledgeable to call in skilled technical help. Preset to react in a general way to an error.

He dug into his mind, trying to remember the faulty light's circuitry. Without looking at the schematic diagrams of it, he knew it was complex, wired into the voltage supply on one hand and into the input signal circuits on the other. A sudden surge in either could cause the light to trip. The operator wouldn't necessarily know which was the source of the error, but a technician such as himself could find out.

He erased Shoshone and now punched in the diagrams of the light. It took him a while to go from general schematics down to specific signal circuits. A voltage-supply error wasn't something the bank would later want to hide, but he felt he should go through the benefit-of-the-doubt motions anyway. No. Money signals—excessive ones—were what he was after.

Like deposits. If an extraordinarily high deposit came in, some sum far out of line with the bank's routine deposits, it would—maybe—trip the light and set up a "false" error condition for the operator. All banks nowadays transferred funds to other banks by computers, moving electronic signals before they actually moved the paper. So that at any given time funds fed by signal to an account in one bank might still be in a bank thousands of miles away. Private jets carrying cargoes of money flew nightly across the country and around the world, trying to keep up with signals that changed accounts at the speed of light. It was a crazy system, a totally mad race, but that's the way it worked. There were people who made hundreds of thousands, even millions, just on the delay between the electronic deposit and the arrival of the paper. *If* the paper ever arrived. Sometimes funds would change banks electronically again, so that nothing would ever show up in the bank for which they were originally intended except another series of signals correcting the first batch.

John thought. If the Shoshone bank's deposit circuits had been preset and then a massive digital word came in, representing money in so large an amount that it looked like an error...what then?

Again he checked the bank's current assets and again got the same figure—just over seven million. It would not be updated until the next morning.

He then checked the previous day's deposits—and was surprised at the number of them, until he remembered that early wheat was being harvested in the Shoshone area and that the bank might be getting a good share of the proceeds.

The deposits came in a long list which the computer automatically broke down, as the many entries would appear illegible on the television screen. On John's second scan, or a portion of it, he found what he was looking for.

Eighty-two million dollars.

It was a preposterously erroneous figure, of course. An error common in the infancy of computer banking, when a signal could come squirting through with dropped decimals, but rare now. Seldom, any longer, did people unexpectedly find themselves with huge balances or with checking accounts mistakenly ten thousand dollars overdrawn. New systems didn't err, or if they did, they quickly corrected themselves.

John almost sighed with relief. The eighty-two-million-dollar signal had obviously triggered a corrective circuit in addition to the error light. The next day the deposit had been erased. There had been no real problem after all.

But then, he thought, frowning, why had Carol the cashier made such a thing out of it?

Or had she? Maybe he'd been wrong about that too; the fact was the girl was a knockout, he'd been about to make a play for her, and his reading of her might have been clouded by his resentment at her quick dismissal of him. The bank *could* have been busy, he insisted to himself again, as simple as that. Maybe he should just drop the whole thing and go home and clean his Sharps—the black powder he used was corrosive and damaging if left in the bore.

Still. It wouldn't hurt just to run a quick check and verify that the huge signal had been spurious and that his own system hadn't somehow kicked out the error. It was, after all, his job, although he couldn't seem to shake the thought that he would be doing something faintly wrong. Not morally wrong, just incorrect, nonfunctional.

He looked at the depositor's code number, which meant nothing to him. But he saved it and ran it back through to identify it in plain language.

And got nothing.

Which was normal. If the signal was incorrect in the first place, there wouldn't be any cross-identification with a person's name. To check further, he put the number through the Shoshone bank's electronic files—and found they had no ID for it. He started to erase and clear and go home when he thought of something else: why not run the number back through his own central data system, and make sure that it wasn't a real deposit from some other account that showed a one-day loss of eighty-two million dollars?

He pumped the number back into central data, waited a second, then stared at the screen, mystified.

The number was still there, it didn't automatically erase, but it was followed by the code symbol for confidential. It had been a real-name account, but a protected one, such as one of the big mega-accounts. That brought up two possibilities. Either the code number for the secret account just happened to be the same code number used for the spurious signal—a coincidence—or money was being hidden in a way he didn't understand.

Except that John had been in logic systems for a long time and knew there was no such thing as applied coincidence. Coincidence was a concept and a tool used in mathematical games; in the real world you had to assume it didn't exist.

There was, when you got to the bottom line, something peculiar going on.

SIX

Systemcheck, phase II

Ten minutes had passed and John was still trying to decide on the best course of action. Lacking the special digital decoding breakdown, he had no easy way to break into the confidential accounts. The computer kept certain data inaccessible to nearly everybody; even he, who was otherwise intimate with the system, could learn only that secret information existed, not how to get at it. At one point in the past, he had heard rumors that certain major bank computers had direct linkage with federal income tax computers, with a system that allowed the banks to get at confidential tax records for any number of purposes. This would of course have been strictly illegal. Curious, John had fished for further news about this alleged linkage and found that very few bank people had the necessary date lines to ascertain if it even existed, let alone to use it. No. It was easy to hide things in a computer. Personal codes were extremely difficult to break, and confidential information was almost beyond the risk of discovery.

But now and then something slipped. A diode

or a chip blew, data would slip through, and somebody watching would get a clue. A hint. Which would incite the voyeur to look for more clues, John thought. He smiled briefly at his vision of a dirty old man intently watching for hot numbers.

He could call in the supervisor. In fact he was *supposed* to do that at this point. Computer crime was growing at a phenomenal rate. Data companies were being robbed left and right; one whole California corporation, for example, had been wiped out by sophisticated thieves who had juggled its accounts through electronic means. Bank data systems were among the most vulnerable. There was a standing order out to all technicians, analysts and programmers to report suspicious computer activity immediately.

With this order in mind, John reached for the conventional landline phone, so that his call to the supervisor wouldn't be taped, as were all communications-net calls. Then he stopped his movement.

"Damn." He said it aloud to the emptily humming data room. "The lady is hiding something and I don't want to tell anybody, and where is the sense in that?" He argued with himself under his breath, in vain. "Damn," he said again, frustrated.

He went back to the screen and savagely punched in the Shoshone code again. Once more, he requested an asset statement and the massive deposit statement. They were the same as before.

What did it mean? Eighty-two million dollars—who had that kind of funding to move around?

Say for the moment that the mistake was in the deposit *command*—not that somebody actually had that sum of money, but that the signal for it could slip through.

What did *that* mean?

He wiped his eyes. Somebody with eighty-two million in a bank wanted to transfer it and hit the wrong button? But the money was there, in Shoshone, and it wasn't being treated as merely a mistake—they were trying to hide it. Jesus, why?

What the hell, he thought, exasperated, I might as well go the whole route. He selected the depositor's code number, "lifted" it electronically from the accounts and once more requested a definition in real-name terms.

ACCOUNT NUMBER CLASSIFIED CONFIDENTIAL.

That was predictable of course, merely a restatement; he'd expected it. But after a full twenty-second delay he saw something that wasn't so predictable. As he was about ready to erase, a new message was suddenly added below the first:

VERIFICATION INFORMATION REQUEST CODE.

This was followed by a series of gobbledygook numbers and letters, never seen before by John. There were no further instructions. Just the statement and what might be the request code itself.

John stared at the screen in amazement. Could the equipment actually be volunteering to give away its secrets? Impossible! But if so, where the hell would the request code go if he punched it in? It hadn't said. He thought. Only one course of action was open to him now. He put the numbers and letters he had been given on memory and fed them into his console with a kind of forlorn hope that they meant something to somebody somewhere—he really had no idea if his own data system or some other system would be responsive to them. The request code, if such it truly was, could have gone anywhere. He realized the foolishness of his act the moment he made it.

Nothing happened.

He waited a considerable time, gazing, ultimately glaring at a screen which continued to show only the code he'd punched on memory-hold, nothing else. The lukewarm cup of coffee in his hand got cold. Finally, John swore. There was nothing to do now but turn the whole case over to the data supervisor—an unimaginative dork named Harvey Wilson. He hated doing that. Nobody called Harvey "Harve"; there wasn't an ounce of human warmth in him. He lived in downtown Denver in a small equipment room that controlled five data centers in the western area—a very sophisticated logic and storage system that was time-shared by God knew how many banks and other businesses. He rarely went out; John doubted that he had a friend in the world. But Harvey was efficient; he could handle this case; that's what he was for. John felt it was time for him to get back to his regular job.

He reached for the landline phone. At that moment it rang. He picked it up. "Data Center."

"I'm calling concerning your apparent interest in confidential accounts...."

"Who is this?" John tried to keep his voice calm, cool, but the edge of his excitement was coming through.

"This is the data control supervisor."

"Where's Harvey? You're not Harvey...."

"I am Mr. Wilson's supervisor. We have a notification code on that account if it is called up. Your station has shown interest. May I help you?"

John paused, thought. What in hell was going on? Since when did the bigwigs sit and monitor notification codes? Since when did they help data process stations? "It was nothing important," he lied, without really knowing why he lied. "The number blipped through on an error and I was just verifying that it was a mistake."

"Explain that, please."

"That's all there is. I saw the number in connection with the Shoshone bank and it seemed out of place so I ran a check."

There was silence on the line. Then the voice said quietly, "Okay. In the future don't waste time trying to verify confidential codes. What is your name, please?"

John paused again, then shrugged. They could find it anyway. "John Smith. What's yours?"

Silence again. Then, "All right, Smith. I suggest you get back to work now." The phone went dead.

John sat back down on his console chair, thoroughly confused. The whole thing was getting out of hand. Hidden deposits, covered mistakes, confidential accounts, a data supervisor's supervisor whom he didn't know. The guy hadn't even told him his name, although what difference did it make? They were all the same. It was turning into a very complicated situation, with his own distinctly memorable name right in the middle of it.

John stretched and rubbed the back of his neck and decided to call it a day. Chewing at the issues involved would accomplish nothing. Maybe a fresh approach would come to him if he slept on it. Besides, he had to clean the Sharps. He looked at the digital readout clock over the console. His relief man was due momentarily.

It would be good to dump the whole goddamn thing for a night.

SEVEN

Systemcheck, phase III

He had called her back before Thursday.

At first, ensconced once more in her penthouse apartment with her regular clients keeping her busy, she had decided not to go back at all. Who needed it? But she couldn't put him or the incident out of her mind. Forty-eight hours later she was romanticizing it. She read poetry a bit. One poem that had always fascinated her was *Leda and the Swan* by W.B. Yeats. It seemed to have something to do with her. It was about Leda, a girl being raped by Zeus, in the shape of a swan. His great wings beat upon her.

> Being so caught up,
> So mastered by the brute blood of the air,
> Did she put on his knowledge with his power
> Before the indifferent beak could let her drop?

That was it. Could she take on what he knew along with what he would be sure to do to her? The challenge excited her. He *exuded* knowledge and power. Truly, it had been like getting screwed by a god. In the end, she had decided to go back on Thursday—to try it at least one more time.

Then he had called. God, he had called, and the flat voice had told her to come on Tuesday instead and she had felt as if she had no choice in the matter. Yes, she had said dully, she could make room on Tuesday for him. Yes, four o'clock in the afternoon was fine.

But it hadn't been fine. Nothing about it had been fine.

At four she had arrived and he'd coldly told her to strip. When she'd protested he'd hit her. Once, but viciously. And she'd taken her clothes off. But there wasn't any romance in it—none at all! He'd made that quadraphonic music come through again and told her to dance and she'd tried, tried to make it work, but her stomach hurt where he'd hit her. The dancing was bad and he'd beat her, systematically, with short chop-blows. Finally, she'd lain on the couch in a ball, and he'd taken her like that. Then he'd stood.

"You'll stay," he'd said. "You can live in the bedroom. I'll tell you when I need you."

It was awful!

When he was done with her—that was what terrified her. Dressed, she sat in his bedroom, dry-eyed but terrified because she knew no way out of the place. She was virtually kidnapped. Her body, to be used again and again by him, was its own ransom! What in God's name had she gotten into? She felt she needed a drink desperately.

It was while in this situation that she first learned of John Smith.

She was listening at the bedroom door,

hoping that somehow she'd be able to make a break for it, when the door buzzer rang. She heard him go and let somebody in. Muffled voices. She pressed her ear to the crack.

"...Goddamn it, man, can't you handle one man on your staff?" He was angry, without being disconcerted, as if whatever the problem, it was well in hand.

"He's just curious. We had a diode blow and some signals went out. We did the repair and rectified the errors, but this one data man got the message as it went through. He checked it out. It's done, I think."

"You think?"

"Well...."

"Thinking isn't good enough. Run a program to verify the corrections have been made and then order a wipe on this...what's his name?"

"Smith. John Smith."

"Christ. All right—order a wipe on this Smith. Get back to me when the job is done. Where does he work?"

"Denver Data Center."

There was a sigh—not sad, but exasperated. "That goddamn diode hit more systems than I thought. I hope this is the last of it."

"It is. I'm sure of it."

There was the sound of the door being closed and she moved away quickly to the bed. She was sitting when he came in.

"You hungry?" He asked it abstractly, the way one might suggest a feeding to livestock. He seemed mostly concerned about her shape. "There's food out on the cart. Go eat."

It was an order and she complied, eating woodenly of some cold chops. She'd heard of these things, heard of prostitutes who had found themselves under slavery conditions and had never been able to understand how they could allow it to happen. She'd always been so in control of her life, of the situations she'd put herself in...and here, she'd let it happen to her too.

She was, almost literally, paralyzed by fear. She could put forkfuls of food in her mouth, but she couldn't make her mind work. Her mental stagnation frightened her as much as the presence of her captor; how *could* she be so frightened?

She had to leave and was afraid to leave, hated to stay and found herself willing to stay. She was hung up like meat on a butcher's hook.

It was as if he could read her thoughts.

She finished eating in three minutes or three hours—time meant nothing to her—and when she was done she continued to sit.

"What's the matter with you?" He came up in back of her and lifted her by the arm up out of the chair. "You act like meat. Well, damn, maybe that's what you are."

He dragged her back into the bedroom. To endure what followed, she had to detach her feelings from her body in a way that she had not done since she'd started out, a nervous tyro in her profession. She waited emptily until he was done. When he was finished he beat her again, angry now that she had not shown more emotion. She didn't even cry; she couldn't; she felt like a dirty common hooker, almost as if she deserved the humiliation he had heaped on her. And would continue to heap on her. She knew that to survive she had to get out. But how?

How do you get out of your life?

"I'm leaving. I'll be back. Be here." He dressed and went out, locking the door behind him. She watched him go, unable to move a muscle. But when he'd been gone a few moments the fear abated somewhat and she found herself standing by the phone. She picked it up, held it a minute, put it down. Who do dirty little hookers call? Who will help a dirty little hooker? She felt she couldn't call a soul she knew.

She took the phone book and almost idly, with no real plan in mind, looked up Denver Data Center. That was the company he'd mentioned. That was where they were going to "wipe" somebody named John Smith. As he was "wiping" her? No, worse; John Smith was going to get wiped without knowing a thing about it, without any of the sense that she had of being an accomplice in her own destruction.

She dialed the number. Maybe she couldn't leave. But she could screw it up for him; she could ball the whole thing up and tell this Smith what was coming.

"Denver Data. May I help you?"

"Mr. John Smith, please."

"One moment, I'll connect you."

"Data control. Smith speaking."

"Mr. John Smith?"

"Yes. Who is this?"

"Look, Mr. Smith, who I am doesn't matter. This is about you. You're in deep trouble because of something called a diode."

"What?"

"That's all I know. Some men are planning to kill you, I think—they used the word wipe—because a diode went out or something. I don't know what it means but I overheard them."

"What are you talking about? Who is this?" John repeated.

"Never mind. Just watch out because I heard they were going to wipe you because...."

She suddenly stopped her babbling. The door was opening and he was back, inside too fast, while she still had her hand on the phone. She slammed down the receiver but it was too late. He was on her, pounding her down, driving her across the floor with lashed kicks. She couldn't count the blows; they were everything, all rolled into one endless pain as he worked at her until he was tired and could beat her no more. At the end, she was no longer even whimpering, just lying still in her agony.

EIGHT

Initial program run

John put the phone back on the hook when he heard the connection go dead. He looked around, feeling aimless.

The technician who had come to relieve him was hung over. He stood at the console with a surly expression on his face, sipping bourbon-laced coffee as an antidote to last night's party, ignoring Smith. He didn't like Smith anyway. He tended to like only the bottle.

John stared at the back of the reliefman's head. Should he tell him what he had just been told on the phone...and the rest of it? He didn't know. He didn't trust the man. He didn't trust anybody he could think of right now.

What the hell is going on, John thought. I don't know anything about something and somebody thinks I know something about something and they are going to—how did the woman put it?—wipe, yeah, they are going to wipe me. Christ. What does *that* mean?

He made a decision to leave the center and take his secret with him. He would figure out what to do later, in the privacy of his home. He left the console room and stood in the hallway for a moment, frowning over his residual doubts at having said nothing to the other technician. He was just getting ready to move off when the door behind him opened again.

"Smith! Oh. You're right here. Lucky I caught you." It was the relief man, speaking sourly. "It's Wilson. He wants to talk to you on the landline."

John moved back into the room and took the phone. "Smith here."

"Ahh, John, I hoped I might catch you still there. It makes it more convenient."

"What's the matter?" John was listening with his pores, all of him alert, like a ground-squirrel just before the bullet takes him.

"Nothing, really." Harvey Wilson's voice was smooth, clean. "I wanted to tell you what the problem was with that diode and why we had that error signal."

Wilson had never called John by his first name before. He'd never bothered to be nice to subordinates. "Thank you." John fought to keep his voice as even as his supervisor's. But all that the woman had said on the phone about his getting "wiped" flooded back into his mind. He was certain he was being set up.

"I can't tell you over the phone. It's rather...uhh...delicate. I thought I might buy you dinner and we could discuss the whole situation at leisure."

"Sure. Why not?" John waited, and when nothing further came said, "Where should we meet?"

"Oh. I'll pick you up there. Would that be all right? I'm about fifteen minutes away right now—calling from my car."

"All right. I'll...oh, damn, I nearly forgot," he went on hurriedly, "I have a couple of things to take care of. It won't take long. Couldn't I just meet you at a restaurant?"

"Well...sure. Of course. I'll meet you in an hour at Lafitte's. How does that sound?"

"First rate." Lafitte's was the best restaurant in Denver. The best in Colorado, as far as that went. "I'll be there."

John placed the phone back on the wall cradle gingerly. "Damn," he muttered.

He didn't know where he'd be in an hour. Wherever it was, he thought, it sure as hell wouldn't be Lafitte's.

"What's up?" The night man turned, yawning. "You get fired?" His voice was hopeful. "Wilson can your ass?"

John said slowly, "I guess you might put it that way at that...."

He left the building on the run. Out in the lot he fired up his truck, then ran over to the guard who had been holding his Sharps for him.

"You thought I forgot it," he said cheerfully.

The guard nodded. "I was worried you had when you barged out like that. I mean, what if you saw a buffalo you just had to kill?" The guard smiled and handed the gun over.

"Thanks. I have a heavy date and I'm in a hurry, that's all," John said. He loped back to the truck, fairly threw the Sharps in the gun rack and was doing the speed limit by the time he'd hit the traffic on Highway 70, the freeway past the technical complex.

He'd gone three miles in the direction of his home when it dawned on him that going there was almost out of the question. They knew where he lived. They could be waiting there for him.

He could go to the police.

There was that. But what would he say? That a bank computer had screwed up, and that he'd gotten a strange call from a woman he didn't know, and that his supervisor was waiting to take him to dinner at the best restaurant in Denver? They'd throw him out of the station.

He could report his suspicions to the state's bank examiners. All states had teams of accountants responsible for the periodic checking of bank's financial records. But the examiners couldn't take direct action even if they saw evidence of crime—could only recommend action. And by the time he got any action recommended it would be too late.

"Damn it—I've got to do *something!*" John jerked the wheel and swore as a station wagon suddenly cut him off. It was the worst time for driving, the rush hour. He glanced at his wristwatch and saw he still had a half-hour before he was expected at Lafitte's. Maybe the smartest thing he could do was get off the freeway and go home after all—just long enough to pick up some clothes. So thinking, he took the next exit and drove on Colfax towards his apartment complex.

They *couldn't* be there yet, he thought; they would be expecting him at Lafitte's. He had a little time, very little, but some.

The hair on the back of his neck went up as he pulled into his parking area and saw a car with a man in it. But the man got out, and he shrugged the feeling off and parked and went up to his apartment. He threw clothes and toilet articles in a suitcase and clamped the lid. Then he sat on the bed for a few moments, not planning ahead in any major way but reacting to his current thoughts as fast as he possibly could.

He had to get out of there now; that's all he knew. He stood with the suitcase and made for the door but stopped for a last look around. That's when he noticed the kludge box.

What John called his kludge box was actually a code simulator he'd built for testing out programs and computer systems. In it, among other things, was a variable frequency oscillator with which he could trigger any computer program in the world, provided he knew the proper code sequence. Nobody knew he had built this box, and indeed it would have been frowned upon, but he'd fooled around and made it early in his data career and it had some sentimental value for him. Now it might have great value for him—he wasn't sure just how, but he felt he might need it, so he took it and made for the door, still unsure of where to go or just why he was going.

The strident ring of the phone stopped him halfway across the living room.

She was less than human now in her pain, operating more on instinct than on thought. He had beaten her badly again, and then he had left her alone on the floor while he went out on another errand. He might or might not have locked the door behind him; she lacked the will to try it.

"God," she whimpered. "Oh, my God."

She went once more to the phone, crawling on

her hands and knees now, since she could no longer stand. The phone book was still open to the data center so she dialed it and asked for John Smith. She was panting hoarsely. The night-duty operator thought she was crying and gave her John's home phone number.

That number had stayed in her mind just long enough for her to dial it. She listened to it ring three, four, five times. She began to cry then, thinking he wouldn't be there. And then she heard the click as John lifted the phone.

"Help," she said. "Help me. Please."

John knew exactly who it was, could feel her pain through the phone. "Where are you?"

"Downtown Sheraton."

"Can you get out? Can you get downstairs to meet me?"

"...I don't know. No. Yes. Yes, I think I can. I will."

"What room are you in? If you're not down at the entrance, the main entrance, in five minutes, I'll come up and get you."

"Twenty-one forty-four." She did not know how the room number had stuck in her mind. Nothing else did. "But I'll make it. I'll...."

"I'm on the way. See you in five minutes."

He hung up and she dropped the phone and went to the door. It was locked, but from the outside, as if he might have been concerned about someone getting in but not at all about her getting out; she turned the bolt and found, dully, that the door opened straightaway.

There was nobody in the corridor. She went to the elevator, pushed the button and waited what seemed an eternity for the doors to open. Her luck held. He wasn't in the car when it arrived, as she halfway expected he would be. It was empty. She rode down, huddled back in the corner, and saw no one until she got to the lobby floor. A young couple was waiting there for the car, and the man moved forward to help when he saw her.

She used the husband story again and she saw the doorman's face go skeptical. Still, he was kind. "Sometimes they turn mean," he said. "We aren't all like that."

She nodded. "My brother will be here soon."

The doorman nodded and behaved as if he believed her every word, which he did not for a moment. He helped her to a couch and went back to ushering people in and out. Some of them stopped to stare at the disheveled, glaze-eyed girl but, with a glance at the doorman's undisturbed countenance, said nothing.

In four minutes the little truck with the camper top pulled up and John jumped out. He went to the doorman. "I'm looking for a woman who. . . ."

He saw her the same time the doorman pointed. "Over there."

"Jesus."

"Yeah. It's a shitty business, ain't it?" The doorman was staring at him in wonderment that this conservatively dressed, rather ordinary-looking young man should be a pimp. John moved to the woman, shocked by her appearance. She had once been beautiful, he could tell that. But she was battered, bruised and swollen now, and on the verge of collapse. He put an arm around her waist and led her out of the hotel.

"God damn! What kind of asshole would do

this?" he said to the doorman. But the doorman, having done his duty as he saw it, shrugged and turned away. Gently, John proceeded with the girl to his truck, got her into the cab, then went around to the driver's side and drove out of the circle drive, all under the doorman's curious stare.

When he got to the street he hesitated before turning right. "You need to go to a hospital."

"No! Take me...take me somewhere. But no hospital."

"But you might be hurt inside. You need a doctor."

She shook her head. "I need...just rest. Please."

"A hospital," John tried again. "You really must go to...."

"No! He'll find us in a hospital. He'll find us if we call the cops. He'll find us if we go home. He knows everything about everything."

She was babbling hysterically, in a manner that normally would have irritated John. But her physical condition moved him to great compassion. And he knew what she meant, knew at least about some mysterious individual's power because he too had sensed it, from the behavior of the computers and the easy way he had been set up by the supervisors. Somebody evil was exercising a tremendous amount of power.

"All right," he said soothingly. "I'll think of something. A motel. We'll go to a motel. Is that all right?"

She nodded, then fell back weakly against the door. John, after a glance to see that she was breathing all right, drove west towards the mountains, until he saw the right kind of motel—one with an office around the back where he could leave her in the truck while he got a room. He had gathered, from her huddled mutterings during the drive, that she was badly frightened lest anybody else but him see her.

Once in their motel room, he put her on the bed and turned the air conditioner down because she was starting to shiver. He put a blanket over her and, when that didn't stop the shivering, added the spread too. Finally she was quiet. When she seemed to be asleep—or in a coma, something he truly feared—he went back out to the truck and brought in his suitcase and the Sharps, along with the kludge box from the glove compartment.

Then he locked the door with the shotbolt and sat down in the chair opposite the bed. Staring at the battered prostitute, he wondered what in the name of God had happened to his life.

NINE

She awoke screaming. Immediately, John was at her side, soothing her, hushing her up lest the motel owner came running and she be terrified further. "It's all right. It's all right. I'm here." He used his voice like a balm and touched her on the hair and hands. "Try and rest. It's all right...."

"Where am I?"

John told her. "You've been asleep for seven hours. You must have been dreaming and screamed."

"Who are you? Oh—I remember." She started to sit up but the pain drove her down. "Where did you say we were?"

"Motel. Don't worry. We're safe."

"No," she said. "Not ever. Not from him."

"Can you tell me what you mean now?"

But she was drifting off again, in a more comfortable sleep now, and this time John stayed on the bed with her, holding her tenderly in his arms until he fell asleep also.

It was six o'clock in the morning when he awakened. He was ravenously hungry and his arm, under her head, was numb. He tried to move it from beneath her and this brought her awake—this time without screaming.

"Good morning," he said. "How do you feel? Sorry. . .stupid question."

She was more alert now. She said, without rancor, "It was. I won't answer. Ohh, Christ, I hurt." She took note of him lying beside her and shrugged, though it hurt her to. "Well, I've come awake this way once or twice before. Could you help me to the bathroom?"

"Sure." John grinned in relief that she was well enough to gibe at him. She even looked better—very pretty, in fact. She had long shapely legs, like an American Beauty rose, it occurred to him, and her tousled hair, falling across her forehead, made her look sweet and vulnerable despite her newly abrupt manner. He let her stand a moment, leaning against him, then guided her to the glass and formica bathroom. She went in alone, and he went back and turned on the early-morning television news. He hoped that somehow there might be something on the news that would help him understand his present situation better, but of course there wasn't. After a time she came out of the bathroom and he moved to help her to the bed.

"No. Let me do it alone."

He nodded but stayed next to her. She had trouble sitting down on the bed, so he took her elbow and helped her. "Is it too soon to ask what happened?" he said then.

"Yes." She stared at the floor. "It is."

"How about your name? You already know mine."

"Barbara," she said. "Barbara Norton."

"Do they call you Barb?"

"Not twice."

John sighed. "This is such a pleasant conversation."

"What do you want?" she said ruefully. "I've been beaten half to death because I called you to warn you." She was really feeling sorry for herself now. "You want me to be chatty?"

"No. Let's start over, all right?"

"Fine."

"Do you think you could eat?"

"I don't know. Yes. I'm hungry. But something soft. I've got some loose teeth. Soup would be all right, I suppose."

"Son of a bitch."

"Yes, he is. But we'll talk about that later. Right now I can't think past the soup."

"All right." John stood. "There's a diner across the street. I'll get some take-out stuff. After we eat we'll talk some more." He started out, then stopped. "Will you be all right alone for a few minutes?"

"Yes. If you're sure we're safe here."

"For now, yes."

"All right. Coffee, too, okay?"

He nodded and left. When he returned twenty minutes later, carrying bags full of food, she was in the tub. The bathroom door was open and steam boiled into the room. He closed the front door.

"Is that you, John?" she called.

"Yeah. Soup's ready when you are."

"Bring me some of the coffee in the tub, will you?"

He reached in the door and held out a cup. When she didn't take it he stepped further in and handed it to her. His eyes were on her, and when he saw her body in the tub he swore.

"What in hell did he use on you?" She was a mass of yellow-blue-black bruises.

"Kicked me around the floor. I tell you, this bastard is something else." She took a sip of the coffee through puffed lips and settled with a sigh into the water. "That's good. And the water feels divine."

"I'll be waiting outside for you," John said, stepping back into the room. He was, in fact, becoming aroused and felt guilty. Here she'd been through hell and trusted him with her body and he couldn't stop the lust from coming. I'm a Goddamn animal, he thought. That's terrible.

But as soon as he sat on the bed he found himself sobering up, thinking of his predicament again. He kept wondering what he was going to do. He knew damn little, nothing about where the threat to his life was coming from, and the woman was the only key he had at the moment to knowing more. He went back to the door. "Barbara?"

"Yes?"

"I know you don't want to talk yet, but we've got to start so I can get to work on this."

"On what?"

"On getting our asses out of this jam, that's on what."

"I don't think we can."

"Still, we've got to try. The truth is I don't know a Goddamn thing about what we're dealing with. I don't even have any good guesses."

"And you think I do?" Her voice from the bathroom was muffled but he could feel the negativeness of it.

"You know his name. What is it?"

"He told me it was Donald Bixby, but that's probably not his real name. They often don't give their real names. Lots of times they don't give any names at all, but that's the one he used when he called."

"What do you mean?"

"About what?"

"They don't give you their real names. Who is they?"

"Different men. I'm a prostitute. Are you telling me you didn't know?"

"Oh. No." John suddenly felt rotten. "I mean, yes. I guess I just didn't want to hear you say it, that's all."

There was silence. Then her voice was curious. "Does it bother you to have your life saved by a hooker?"

"Don't be stupid."

He could almost see her smile knowingly. "Does it change how you feel about me?"

"No," he lied.

"You're lying."

"Only a little."

He heard her laugh, and he smiled. "Well, hell, I just didn't want to think of it. I thought maybe you just had some kind of special relationship with this guy Bixby. . . ."

"You can say that again. It was special, all right."

"Yeah. But I mean—oh, hell, forget it." Coloring angrily, he strode to the bathroom door, leaned on the jamb looking at her, and started arguing with himself. It doesn't matter. What difference does it make what I think? That doesn't change our predicament at all. He spoke directly to her now: "Let's go back and talk about this guy—what's he like, other than sadistic?"

She thought, then shook her head. "I don't think I can help you with that."

"You don't *think* you can," he exploded. "All right. What did he talk about? Can you tell me that?"

Again she hesitated, "Some man came and told him about you getting curious about something. I don't remember exactly what."

"Money," he said. "I was getting curious about eighty-two million dollars. But I was about ready to drop it when you phoned."

"I guess they didn't know that. Anyway, that's when Bixby said to have you wiped. That's how he put it. Wiped. I just figured you were going to get killed and I felt if I warned you it would be a way of getting back at him."

"Thanks for the feeling."

"I'm trying to be honest." She flushed. "I didn't know you from Adam's asshole, sweet cheeks."

He winced. "Why didn't you try harder to get out of there and save yourself first, rather than me?"

She thought for a long time while she washed her back with a sponge.

"I wanted to hurt him—I still do," she said at last, slowly. "He's...bad. He's a really evil person. But so am I, you see. There's something wrong with me, something sick, and he seemed to know about it so that he could take advantage of it. And...." Her voice broke off. She began to sob quietly.

"Easy. Easy." John was thinking rapidly, not

quite mindless of her feelings but almost. "Some part of you...not all of you, but in some nook and cranny of your soul—you like to get beaten, isn't that it?"

She sniffled. "Maybe."

"Not maybe. That's it." John grew excited. "That's the logic of the situation between you—that's all there is to it. It was clear to him, if not to you. It was his clarity of mind, knowing himself, knowing you, that gave him power over you. He worked you like a computer terminal. Wow!"

She looked at him wonderingly. "It's as if you've forgotten what he did to me, what he's threatened to do to you, as if you didn't care...."

"Of course I care!" John snapped. "That's not the point. I care about my perceptions too. Damn it, I'm interested in them—and I'm interested in *him*, whoever he is! At least, I have something to go on...some basic way of looking at him...somewhere to start."

He sat in the chair next to the bed and stared through a kiddie cartoon show while he continued to think. She finished bathing, came into the room and dressed quietly, watching his excitement decay as he remained, for all his thinking, at step one. Somewhere out there was a logic systems wizard—his equal, his better, he did not know. The man was coming on as omnipotent, was a dire threat to him, but he still didn't know enough to do anything about him.

"It's sure quiet out here." Barbara looked idly out the window, then, finally, back at him. "Do you think maybe you'll come up with a solution? I mean, just something sensible we can do right now?"

"Yeah," he said, depressed. "I'm going to call in the tooth fairy."

She sighed. "While we're waiting for him to come get us, do you think I might have some of that soup now? Cold as it no doubt is. . . ."

He smiled tiredly and got up to eat with her, munching on chicken drumsticks and potato salad while she sipped noodle soup slowly from the styrofoam container he'd brought it in.

"How's it going?" he said, watching her use her lips gingerly.

"Better." She nodded. "And you?"

He shook his head. "I thought about going to the police, but I'm not sure what good it would do."

"I don't like cops."

"The bank examiners are out, because all I could tell them would be a mistake had occurred. The mistake's been fixed. There's nothing legally wrong going on. . . ."

"Then why did they want to kill you?"

"I don't know. I really don't have the slightest idea. Maybe it's my breath." The joke didn't work. It just sounded pathetic.

"That leaves us with nothing," she said, ignoring it.

He nodded. "Almost."

"What do you mean—almost? Do you have something?"

He went over to the TV, cut off the sound and started pacing. "I've been thinking. The way it is now they have it all. We don't know how many other people are controlled by our Mr. Bixby, what their functions are, where they'll be coming from. We're not even sure of Bixby's goal. There's no specific thing we can do with a sense of security...right?" He stopped and looked at her, as if for confirmation.

She nodded.

"But also, short of actually being dead, we can't be one hell of a lot worse off, right?"

Another nod.

"So what if, rather than do any one thing, we go ahead and do everything?"

"What do you mean? I don't follow you."

"Back in the army I used to shoot pool a lot." John smiled. "We used to have a phrase when all the balls were crowded together so that you didn't have one good one to aim at. We used to holler 'shoot hard and holler shit, something's gotta drop.'"

"So?"

"So let's do that now. Let's smash all the balls. We'll call the law *and* call the bank examiners and rattle up all the hell we can. Something's gotta drop, right?"

She looked dubious. "I don't know. They could all drop, right on us."

John argued, "But it beats hell out of just sitting here waiting for something to happen, doesn't it?"

"Do you really need my approval?" She regarded him silently, speculatively.

He thought a moment, looking at her. "Well, sure I do. You're in this like me, aren't you?"

She nodded. Her uncoiffed hair, falling down around her face, made her look helpless and small. "I just want to make sure you really want to do what you're suggesting."

"Damn right I do. Let's start popping caps on the bastards." Smiling tightly, John grabbed the phone. "We'll call the cops first. Maybe they'll give us protection."

She laughed.

"What's so funny?" He was holding the phone up, listening to the dial tone.

"It'll be the first time a prostitute ever got protection from the law without paying for it up front."

He smiled without being aware that he was smiling and dialed the number. When her hair was spilled down that way and she sat all huddled up with trust for him in her dark, puffed-up eyes, he had a difficult time remembering that she was a prostitute.

TEN

The police didn't come. Or at least they weren't the first to arrive. That was the first indication John had of the size and quality of the network controlled by Donald Bixby.

He'd called in and all but demanded that a detective in the larceny division drive out to the motel. He wanted more than a patrolman, he wanted someone with clout. He explained that he and Barbara found themselves in great danger because of a possible bank crime.

What he overlooked in making his report was that all incoming police calls were routinely taped, with their pertinent data fed into the police computer by a key operator. In seconds the officer called can check out in depth the person he is talking to.

And so can anybody else keyed into the police computer system.

John spoke to a Lieutenant Hickson, a conscientious young officer who sat hunched over the phone, making his own notes. "Where'd you say you are now?" Hickson asked, pencil poised over a pad.

John told him again. The name of the motel was recorded both by Hickson and the computer tape, the latter keyed in by John's social security number. Which was to say that anybody waiting for that number to appear in the computer system would merely have to have a program preset: when the number appeared, so, instantly, would the present location of its owner.

"I'll be there in ten minutes," Hickson told John and hung up.

"He'll be right here," John told Barbara, hanging up.

"Subject is at the Cozy Corner Motel, room nine," a man in Dallas said into a microphone. The man was stationed at a trunk computer being shunted into the Denver police computer data by way of Maryland, where the main data control center for national police activity was located. He was feeding the information on to Los Angeles, where another computer operator was waiting for it. This operator's job was to punch the information out to two operatives who were waiting to act on it in Denver. The two operatives had a faster car and were closer to John than the police. They were on their way to the Cozy Corner Motel as John moved from hanging up the phone to sit on the bed next to Barbara. He felt and looked tense.

"So now we wait some more," she said, managing a wry grin in an effort to help him relax. She felt tense herself.

"True," John said. "But for the cops now."

"Story of my life," she said, shrugging. "I always seem to be waiting for the cops."

"Ha!" It was a short burst meant to cover his embarrassment. Every time she hinted plainly at her occupation it got to him in complex ways. He just wished she wouldn't do it so much.

"Cops aren't all that hostile towards you," he argued, angry with her. "It's all in your head. When they come, you'll see...."

Then, abruptly, he trailed off, staring at the floor.

"What's the matter?"

"Nothing...."

"Now you're lying."

"Yeah. I sure am," he breathed. "Look, I might be a little paranoid myself. Maybe I've caught it from you. Let's get out of here."

"*What?*"

"We're leaving. Right now. Get dressed."

"For God's sake, why? You just called the cops...."

"Yeah. And anybody else on the line, too. That's what's suddenly bothering me. It was bugging me while I was on the phone too, but I couldn't pin it down. Come on, move! We might not have much time."

She got up and started to get her things together. She was incredulous. "You mean you think he's got all the cops, too?"

"Not necessarily. But if his operation is as big as it sounds so far, he might have a tap into their computer."

"But they'd know...."

"No. He could slide it in and they'd never know. It's done all the time. And if he's done it he could have found out where we are as soon as the police did. I was talking to that Hickson lieutenant for at least fifteen minutes after I let him know we're here. I think—"

John broke off because there was a knock on the door. He went to the side window and peeked out through the crack in the curtain.

"There are two of them," he whispered.

"Cops always come in pairs," Barbara said.

"Maybe." He turned to the door and called loudly. "Who is it?"

"Police. May we come in? We're here in answer to your call."

"What's your name?"

"Pederson. Pederson and McWilliams. Come now, Mr. Smith, open the door."

"It's a setup," John hissed to Barbara. "I know it is. Hickson said he'd be here himself."

He looked around desperately. There was no back window to exit from. "Damn. No way...." His eyes fell on the Sharps' case in the corner. He'd brought the rifle in but the cartridges were still in the glove compartment of the truck. No. He had a small case of ten in his suitcase that he'd thrown in when he was packing. A case of elk loads—no reason for them to be there except that he had in mind running to the mountains when he'd run. Always run to the country—it was what the old mountain men said. Run to the hills when things were backing you up.

He pulled the case off the Sharps, which still hadn't been cleaned from firing. The smell of sulphur cut the room.

"God, what is that thing—a cannon?" she asked.

"Buffalo gun," he said. "Bull gun."

He rummaged through the suitcase and found the cartridges.

"Christ," she said, "what if it *is* the cops?"

"It's not." He loaded the rifle, pulling the lever up with a smooth snick. Then he moved off to the side of the door. "All right. You open it and as soon as you do, drop on the floor," he whispered to Barbara. "Stay down until I tell you to get up."

She nodded. "I hope this works."

"So do I." His hands were steady on the rifle despite his fear. He swung the barrel up to the opening edge of the door. "Go."

Barbara pulled the chain back and unlocked the door. "Come in," she said, and dropped to her knees.

Any doubt John may have had concerning the two men was dispelled the moment the door opened a crack. They slammed into it and powered into the room with their shoulders, side by side, thinking they had surprise on their side.

But she was beneath them and they tripped on her and John was off to the side. When they got straightened halfway around and started to get up they were looking down the bore of the bull gun. It was like a tunnel. "Move and I'll kill you."

"With that thing? You're kidding." This from the one on the right. "That's an antique."

"Smell the barrel." John slammed the end of it in the man's nose so hard it started to bleed. "Smell the powder?"

The man didn't say anything, but he didn't move any more, either. His partner leaned back against the wall, relaxed but not too relaxed. He was ready, a pro.

"Get up, Barbara," John told her. "Search them. Off to the side so I have a clear shot."

She did so and came up with two snubnose pistols and several thousand dollars in fifties and hundreds. No identification. No wallets.

The money was in envelopes.

"I don't suppose your names matter anyway," John said, shrugging. "You working for Bixby?"

It was worth a try, but neither of them showed any sign of knowing the name. They simply sat quietly, waiting their chance.

"Give me the guns," John said to Barbara. She handed them over. He broke one open and dropped the cartridges on the floor. They were .38 Special wadcutters. "Nasty. You guys are serious about this, aren't you?" He was doing it more or less as he'd seen it done in the movies, trying to put off his mortal fear with a forcefully calm act. But then he couldn't suppress his rage. "Fucking bastards."

He turned to the second handgun, first checking to make sure it was loaded. Then he aimed it at the two men and handed the Sharps to Barbara. "Put this in the truck. In the back. Then wait in the cab for me."

"What are you going to do?"

"Nothing. Go."

She did as he said and he looked at the men. "Get up. Slowly. With your hands on your head and your backs to me."

They complied, but tried to move apart and split his attention.

"No. Back together. I will definitely shoot you, both of you, if you give me a reason."

There was that unsure edge in his voice and they believed him because of it—he was frightened enough to shoot.

"Get in the closet," he said.

"It won't hold us," the one on the left said flatly. He was trying to upset John into dropping his defenses.

"Get in the closet," John repeated, "*now*." He stepped forward and gave the one who had talked a sharp tap under the ear with the gun barrel. The man brought his hand up in pain. "I'm getting pissed off at you guys," John said.

They got in the closet and he closed and locked the door. Then he pulled the bed over against the closed door, knowing it wouldn't help a hell of a lot but hoping it might slow them down.

He ran outside with his suitcase, saw their car next to the truck and paused long enough to open the hood and jerk out all the distributor wires. Then he joined Barbara in the cab. Backing the truck up, he told her what he'd done.

"They'll break out of that closet soon enough and I want to be gone from here before they do. The way I feel, I'd kill the bastards," he swore at her.

She saw the murder near to blazing in his eyes and the pressure he was under fighting to restrain it. "Then you're making a smart move," she said. "You're no killer—I don't want you to kill anybody." He felt the warmth of her sympathy and affection spread over him. It gradually calmed him. "Only, where to now?" she added quietly.

He shrugged as he turned onto the highway and headed towards Denver.

"Hell, if the mountain doesn't come to you, you go to the mountain, right? We'll go down and talk to Hickson in person."

"Mr. Smith, I'm afraid we have a little

problem on our hands." Hickson's neck was stiff. He was a big, burly cop, and he rubbed his neck with a hand that looked like a ham.

"You didn't go up to the motel at all, did you?" John said accusingly. He was talking to the lieutenant at police headquarters. "We drove straight from there to here and I halfway expected to meet you on the road. But damn it, two people tried to kill me up there, and I don't believe you got off your butt!"

Hickson looked at him stonily. "I didn't go, if that's what you mean. We did a little checking on you before we moved on your call. We ran your name through the system." He looked up as if that explained everything.

"So?" John waited impatiently. "You ran a check. So why didn't you come?"

Barbara said, "Did somebody high up tell you not to, lieutenant? You see, John thinks there might be a conspiracy under way to—"

"No." Hickson sounded both impatient and tired. He didn't like explaining. Sometimes he thought that's all cops did. Explain. "Goddamn it, what do you two think this is—some kind of game? I've got real people out there who are really getting robbed, real crime. I don't have time to play around—look, Smith, I called your supervisor after the computer check. He verified it all."

"Verified what?"

"That you have...problems. Our computer showed the four times you were involved in false crime reporting—being a buff, looking for excitement and all. Why don't we just drop it? I'll let you two split for now because no real harm was done. But the next time I'm going to hang your ass, understand?"

"It's a setup," John said, nodding. "Look, I know you're not going to believe this, but what they did was cross-feed your computer with false information about me to throw you off."

"That's off, Smith, way off. Our crime computer isn't even here. It's back in Maryland. They couldn't go all the way back there and...ahh, hell, now you've got *me* doing it."

"No. They did it. They can do it on any telephone. It takes just seconds. They fed incorrect data in on my name so you wouldn't act on any call from me. Don't you see? They couldn't put anything really bad in because then you'd check and find that it was phony—especially if I got arrested and had to go to trial. But something like this—something to just throw you off."

Hickson looked at John for a long time. Some of these Goddamn liars were so much in earnest you could hardly believe they were lying to you, even when you *knew* they were. There was only one way to handle them; sternly.

"Look, Smith, let me put it this way. If you aren't out of the building in five minutes I'm going to kick your ass until it's a ring around your neck."

"Come on, John," Barbara said, standing up. She knew about cops. "It's over. He isn't going to help."

"What happened to your face, lady?" Hickson was professionally curious. "Some trick work you over?"

"Stick it, Hickson."

"Yeah, yeah, yeah. Get the hell out of here. I've got work to do." He went back to some papers on his desk.

"Come on, John." Barbara repeated. She took his arm firmly and aimed him toward the exit. "Police stations are not good places to hang around in."

John went along, shaking his head. He was quiet until they were outside in the parking lot. Then he blew up in anger. "Of all the goddamn bullshit—that man didn't believe me. He wouldn't listen to me at all."

"Ahh, Hickson's all right. I've seen worse. He's just tired or something."

"But damn it, Barbara. . . ."

"No. It's over. Forget it. Now we're on our own—that's the way it always is when you try dealing with cops. You wind up on your own."

He stopped before they got to the car and looked at her with sudden new interest and understanding. "It's like this for you all the time, isn't it?"

She gave a short, bitter nod without turning. "You've got that right."

"You're always outside of everything, aren't you?"

"I said yes, didn't I?" She turned and he could see the anger in her eyes. "And I like it that way. There was a time when I wanted all the polyester and diapers and stability you keep hearing about as good things. But no more. The way I live now, the way I chose to live, I like what I have—I just get pissed off when I have to go and talk to the cops and find out how it is between me and them all over again. I always realize I should have known better."

John didn't say anything but followed her with a comprehension he hadn't known before.

It was incredible, he thought, that he hadn't known before about what hookers—prostitutes, he corrected himself—were up against. Not to know about a culture within his own everyday world that couldn't use the law or the social structure it lives in. Christ, what an astonishing way to live!

The way I live now. The thought burned into his mind. The way *I* live now.

"Wait for me," he said, and caught up with her as she got to the truck.

ELEVEN

It was after noon when they pulled back onto the street from the police parking lot. Denver was, as usual for the time of year, hot and smoggy; the yellowish air came down on them like a smothering blanket.

"Jesus," she said. "Don't you have air conditioning?"

"No. I always get colds from the things, so I never got one. Roll your window down."

She did so, but even with both windows down the movement of air didn't do much to cool them. He could see perspiration forming on her breasts above the low-cut shift, and he knew his own face glistened with it. Summer prairie heat is murder in the city.

"Should I say it, or do you want to?" She turned to him.

"Say what?" he asked.

"What in hell do we do now?"

He laughed but there was no humor in it. "I've been thinking about that ever since the cop said he was going to kick my ass up around my neck."

"And?"

"I don't know."

"That's great. Just great."

"Just being honest."

"So next time lie."

They drove in silence for a while, each thinking, and after several blocks they turned to each other simultaneously.

"I've got an idea...."

"We could...."

They smiled. "Hell," John said, "I was just shooting in the dark. You tell me your idea first."

"I was doing the same thing. I don't have an idea." She shrugged. "I was going to say we could go somewhere and hope that this all blows over. Or something."

John laughed. "It must be the animal instinct to hide. I was going to say the same thing. But it won't work."

She nodded again. "I know."

"So."

"So."

"So shit," she said.

"Yeah. All right. Let's start out by establishing a negative logic base."

"Whatever in hell that means." She looked out the window, disgusted. She hated pretentious people and she thought that's what he was becoming. And just when she was starting to kind of like him, too.

"Sorry. I'm sounding like an ass. I just mean, let's start out by figuring out what it is we *can't* do—maybe an idea will come to us."

"We can't go to the cops," she suggested.

He nodded. "Agreed. And we can't go home—I mean we can't go to my place or your place. They have both addresses by now, from the computer link with the police data system."

"I wonder why they don't just have us busted?" She turned to him. "I mean, if they can take information out of the computer and they can put it in, why don't they just say we're murderers or something, and have us arrested? Wouldn't it be easy for them?"

He nodded. "I thought about that for a while. But it wouldn't serve their purpose to have us in jail."

"What do you mean?"

"Having us inside won't do them any good. If we're on the outside they can deal with us the way they want to deal with us."

"You mean kill us."

"Yes." He turned onto the freeway north.

"I've never had anybody try to kill me before. I mean really, seriously, work at trying to kill me. Have you?"

"Yes."

She turned to stare at him, long and hard. Finally, she asked, "You were in Viet Nam?"

He nodded. "I was outside of Da Nang for four months. On the edge of the bush." Firebase Alpha came back and the incomings and the stink of the flatcrack that came and came and came all the time. So many were dead or would be dead. But it wasn't like this—there wasn't thought behind the artillery. Only mechanically impersonal death. Here there was thought, presence—a man wanted them dead. Personally.

"Was it—it it scary all the time like I'm scared now?"

He thought about how, after a lengthy barrage, all the men compared pants full of shit; about how men just sat down and cried in the dirt, with nobody thinking that crying was strange. "It was . . . different. In a way this is worse because it's so directed; in a way that was worse because it was so impersonal."

"Have you ever shot anybody? Killed anybody?"

"I don't know."

"Right." There was scorn in her voice.

"No. I don't. Like you said, I'm no killer. But I shot a lot and tried to hit people, but you never know if you do. Some go down, some don't. Everybody's shooting. You never know." He sighed, tucked the little pickup in back of a semi as they went around the shallow turn past the Denver football stadium and on out of the city, north, towards Wyoming. "Look. I'd rather not talk about Nam if it's all right. It was all bad and it doesn't do us any good anyway. Let's get back to work on our problem."

"Which was, we can't go home and there's some guy wants to kill us." She sat up, winced a bit with the pain in her side. "Where are we going now?"

"North. You all right?"

"I hurt but I'm getting better, I think. What's north?"

"Wyoming."

"God."

"It's not so bad. We can find a place and hole up and work out some kind of plan of action."

She said nothing and sat looking out the side window, and after a time he realized she was crying. As they drove through the smoke of industrialized Commerce City, past the oil storage tanks into the north prairie that was somehow more old-west than the eastern prairie, great tears were working down her cheeks.

"I don't see that we have any choice," he said, trying to placate her. "If we stay in Denver, Bixby will just send those two goons at us again."

"Damn it, I'm all right." She shook her head. "I didn't cry for years and years and now in two days I'm bawling *all* the Goddamn time—look at me!"

John smiled. "So cry. What the hell, I used to do it all the time."

"Whores don't cry."

"Don't...," he started, then stopped. Shook it away.

"Don't what?"

"Nothing."

"Don't call myself a whore, is that what you were going to say?"

He didn't say anything, stared down the freeway intently.

"Don't work my case, John."

"I'm not."

"Don't. You don't understand anything, you know what I mean? I like what I am and when I want to change I'll let you know, all right?"

He nodded. "You got it."

"All right then."

"All right."

"Let's change the subject, shall we? Pray for peace and all—an armistice."

She smiled. "Yeah. Sorry. What do you want to talk about?"

"You're kidding—how about the weather? Or books? Seen any good movies lately?"

"Do you honestly have any idea what we're

going to do?" She looked from the road to his face, then back to the road. "Any idea at all?"

He paused, then shrugged. What the hell. Might as well be honest. "No. I'm just driving north and living a day at a time—a minute at a time. Hoping something will come to me. I just wish I knew what in hell Bixby is so pissed off about."

"Some kind of error or something. That's all I heard. He said it was a big operation and there was an error—something like that. My brain is still a little scrambled from the beating. Damn. He really worked me over." She shuddered, remembering. "But he thinks you know about the error. I think."

"All I know is that a mistaken deposit of eighty-two million dollars was made to the Shoshone Bank—just squirted through and then was taken off the books. It happens all the time. Well, not all the time, but pretty often."

"Eighty-two million," she said slowly. "That's a lot of money."

"Not really. Big banks deal in hundred-million blocks now, and billions. The oil companies are into trillion dollar deals. Eighty-two million isn't much to some of those people. That's what I don't understand—I don't know what I saw. If I just knew what the error meant, what I'd seen, then maybe we could come up with some kind of plan. I don't know...."

"We have error ramification failure on two levels," the data man in Los Angeles reported on the com-net to the western subcontroller in the Denver terminal, the information cycling through and being monitored by the Dallas main data center. "Please inform control."

"Standby one." The terminal operator in Denver pushed a hold button on the com-net unit. "I'll bring control up on a landline and patch him in."

The operator did not know control, did not know Bixby at all, but knew his power—he was the boss. She called a number she had for control contact, was held while a second number was patched through and Bixby came on.

"Control, we have a landline patch ready to go with Los Angeles."

"Go ahead." Bixby sounded bored. "Scramble it."

"Very well." The terminal operator hit a scramble switch that, for security purposes, coded everything that was said. "You are scrambled."

"We have error ramification failure on two levels," the data man repeated to Bixby. "I'm keeping you informed as per instructions."

"What are the two levels?" Bixby knew one—John Smith—but was testing the validity of the system.

"Subject 2011 in the northern oil fields was ordered eliminated. The order was a mistake but the attempt was carried out and the subject escaped. He is still not located although the general area is of course known."

"And the second error?"

"In Denver. Subject 2012. Through the same error—the blown diode—classified information went through his system. He might have seen it and the order to eliminate went out automatically, as per program stipulation. It was all covered by the existing security programs. Somehow the operatives malfunctioned...."

"Somehow."

"....Yes, somehow, and the subject was allowed to escape, along with a woman. The two are currently driving north on I-70 and being followed by the backup operative assigned as per security programs. The operative picked them up at the police station when the shunt notified us that they were there."

"So there's really no problem," Bixby said.

"No sir. None. All contingencies are covered, as I said, in existing programs. All other errors have been rectified and these two will be shortly. We're just keeping you posted as you instructed."

"Very well. Inform me as soon as both errors have been rectified."

"Of course."

There was the click of com-nets being disengaged and the quiet shuff-whistle of them being cut down.

"All this time in Colorado, and I never got up to Wyoming," Barbara said, as they crossed the state line. "Now I know why. Jesus." She stared out at the Wyoming flats, the incredible distances that seem to go forever.

"It's all in what you like," John said, grinning. "I think it's fantastic. Sometimes I come up here to hunt mule deer and I just go and go, on foot, back up into the foothills. You have to get into it to really understand it. Just imagine," his voice was light, as enthused as a boy's, "when people like us first came here they were on horses, or in wagons with oxen; the nearest neighbor might be over a week away."

She looked at him. "You'd like that, wouldn't you? To go back to those old days?"

He smiled. "Yep. When I grow up I want to be a cowboy. No—not that. But I'd like to...to go back to when it was simple. When they didn't know so much about you. When there weren't computers."

She turned back to the landscape, tried to look at it with interest, failed. "I agree with that, about computers. But I like refrigerators and some TV and lots of modern cities. I'm not sure I could get along too well without them."

"That's too bad."

"Why?"

"Because doing without them is exactly what we're going to do when we hole up."

"Oh, good," she said, frowning. "I might have known. Somehow that figures."

John smiled without further comment. As they drove north, the traffic had thinned. He leaned back and relaxed while he drove. Happy about getting into wide open country, he'd almost forgotten the medium-to-high probability of pursuit. He began to study the mirrors carefully to see what traffic was behind him.

A full mile in front of John, the standby operative looked into his mirror and deftly matched his car's speed with the small yellow truck in the rear.

Fifty-five. Fifty-seven. Just right.

There was no hurry. There would be plenty of time to do the job right; the last team had hurried, and look what it got them. Do things right the first time and then they didn't back up on you.

He nudged speed up a bit, then dropped back. Plenty of time. Just hold the same distance until he found out what was going on; what the subject had in mind by running north.

Beneath the dash of the car was a mobile phone. He reached down and plucked it out and reported back to data control. Every fifteen minutes. Keep everybody informed.

There was no hurry.

TWELVE

In Casper, Wyoming, John pulled into a mall shopping center and killed the engine. It was late afternoon and the drive up had been uneventful; long, stifling hot, but uneventful.

"We have to get outfits," John said, turning in the seat. "You want to wait in the car and trust me to buy you clothes?"

"Do I look awful?" She reached up and turned the rearview mirror. "I look awful," she said, nodding. "Give me a minute to fix up. Do you have a comb?"

She had no purse, no makeup, and still looked pounded on, but some of the eye swelling was going down. She combed her hair out, long and black and rich, and brought it down to hide the bruises on her cheeks. "Now how do I look?"

"Stunning—stunningly awful."

"Why did your mother let you live?"

He laughed. "You look fine. Let's go in."

"We don't have any money, do we?"

"We'll use my credit cards. What the hell, if we make it, I'll be glad to pay it. If not, it won't matter. Right?"

"Don't talk that way."

"Sorry." He got out of the truck. "Come on—let's go shopping."

He bought her jeans, shirts, underwear, then walking boots for both of them—not what he thought of as those silly newfangled boots, but good supple crepe-soled boots that took your ankle and held it while you walked. He also bought light windbreakers, a hunting knife for him, compass, backpack, small cooking gear, sleeping bags, a tent and other general camping needs.

Then they went to the supermarket and bought what looked to Barbara like a month's supply of food for a small army. It took four carts to ship it all out to the truck.

"Where the hell are we going?" she demanded, looking at the stack of goods. "And for how long?"

"Up in the mountains," John said. "For as long as it takes to come up with a plan. You got any better ideas?"

"No. I just don't want to grow old here."

They got in the truck and John went to gas up at the mall's Exxon station. He put it on a different credit card. "I suppose they'll have another computer shunt into all the credit computers," he said, while the man was filling the truck. "But the worst they'll find out is we're in Casper—they won't know where we've gone."

"Neither will I. And I'll be there."

"You'll love it. Just wait." He wheeled out onto the freeway and headed north again. "I've hunted deer in this country and it will do us just fine. It's isolated and clean and open and...well, good for your mind. Back when I first got out of the veterans' hospital I came up here sometimes and it helped me quite a bit."

"Were you wounded?"

He hesitated. "Sort of..." He started to say more but stopped. "It doesn't help to talk about it." Flatcrack of death, hotsplat of fire all the time, until there was no thought, no thought at all until the white rooms of the hospital brought peace and quiet. He decided to tell her the truth. "I was shook up in the head, is what."

She nodded but didn't push it and he was glad. "How far to this place we're going to hole up in?" she asked.

"About eighty miles—but distances out here are deceptive."

"How so?"

"The first thirty miles on the freeway going northwest take about thirty minutes. The next fifty are on twin ruts that go back into the foothills and up in the mountains and that will take damn near seven hours. If, that is, we don't have to stop and clear the road of rocks or fallen trees."

"But it's late. That will make it dark when we get in."

"No. It will be light. We'll be camping along the way tonight, then arrive in the morning. There's a place I know where we can stop and take some evening trout for this great supper I'll make you...."

"I wondered why you bought that fishing stuff."

"Not stuff. That was a Pfleuger fly rod and reel with assorted flies I bought. Very good equipment. Also very expensive."

"Sorry." She was teasing. "Pardon me for living."

"Just trying to help you through your first

trying days out here...."

"I was never any good at being a jock." She smiled. "I was really only good at one thing."

"Yes. Well." He reddened and she laughed.

"You keep forgetting what I do for a living."

"Yes. I do."

"Does it still bug you?"

"A little. I have some growing to do. I'll get over it."

"I hope so. We're stuck together for a while, the way it looks. We'll have to accept each other."

"God," he sighed. "It's so strange."

"What?" She bristled. "Accepting me?"

"No, no, not that. All of this. One day I'm sitting there, playing with my computer, and the next day a woman calls and saves my life and I've got people trying to kill me and I don't even know why. It's just crazy. It's like I don't know how I got involved in my own life—like watching a movie of me."

"It is a little weird," she said. "When you think of it."

"I never asked you—how did you get involved with Bixby?"

"Uhhh...work. He came highly recommended. By a judge in...some other place."

John whistled. "Talk about blowing a recommendation."

She said nothing.

"Does it...happen often? That they turn sour on you like that?"

She looked at him. "One rule all hookers follow—never talk about tricks, all right?"

John's face reddened again. "Sorry, I don't know a whole hell of a lot about the ethics of your profession."

She laughed. "You sure blush easy. Especially for somebody who was in the army."

"I always have. Must be my blood is close to the skin—that's what my mother used to say all the time."

"How come you're not married? Man like you with a good job ought to be married."

"I was."

"Oh. Any kids?"

"No."

"I guess you don't want to talk about that, right?"

"You got it." He frowned, then laughed. "It was nothing at all, my marriage. Nothing to talk about. Nothing worked. Like a tired horse." He looked up ahead. "There's our turn—exit eighty-seven."

She stared out the window. There was an off ramp that went up and crossed a gravel road that went out of sight in both directions. There were no buildings, no other signs of human life; just the road. East into the plains, west up into some hills in the distance which she knew would ultimately lead to mountains, though they were still lost in the evening's heat haze. "Why is there a road here at all?"

"About fifteen miles east there are two ranches. West about fifty miles there used to be some mines but they're all closed down. The road isn't maintained, but if you're careful, and don't mind pulling a rock or two, you can get back in there. It's private except during deer season when a few four-wheelers come up here to hunt. But not too many come even then—the better deer places are up further north."

John signaled and turned off on the ramp. "Now we get some country," he said. "Real country."

"Oh good."

He laughed. "You'll love it. Really. Don't worry."

"God*damn*!" The operative let the car slow of its own accord so that there wouldn't be any brake lights showing. He watched carefully in the mirror. All that driving through flat country had numbed him, he'd grown complacent. He could see now that the subject had turned off the freeway behind him. He had to turn around and go back.

"Damn." He swore again, but with less heat, alert now to this fresh aspect of his job. He looked both ways, made sure there were no police cars on the horizon, then drove across the median to the southbound lane and sped back to the exit. He drove up the opposite ramp from the one the subject had taken.

He stopped at the top and watched the small truck heading west in the distance. A plume of dust was coming up from the back wheels, like an arrow pointing out a cloudy trail into the evening sun. After a moment of study he frowned, picked up the mobile phone and called in.

"Subject has turned off on exit eighty-seven onto a gravel road," he reported. "Lots of dirt kicking up off of it. Close following could be risky. Please advise."

"Where does the road go?" subcontrol asked. He was in Los Angeles working through Dallas on the same patch used for the previous calls.

The Denver terminal lacked decision-making capabilities, and main control didn't want to be bothered until the job was finished.

"It's not on the maps. It's just an old gravel road—secondary and not very well maintained, from the look of it."

"Can you follow at all?"

"Affirmative. But only at a great distance. Plus it's getting dark."

"Evaluate."

"I can keep on following, but I request that a doubled risk factor be entered until dark. Please key in all my data and advise immediately."

"Standby one." There was a pause while subcontrol ran a probability pattern. "Follow. The risk is well within limits due to the remoteness of the area you are in. The prospects of elimination without outside interference are excellent, on the order of 500-to-1. Any further requests?"

He looked down the road at the darkening sky and the disappearing truck. He had an impulse to add to the data the fact that he had no food along, but thought better of it. That was, he realized, a kind of joke he was using to ward off his general anxiety. Subcontrol never keyed in jokes. "Negative. I will report in regularly."

"Of course." Subcontrol's voice was just slightly acid. "As per instructions."

"As per instructions."

He hung up the phone and sat, waiting for the yellow truck to disappear completely. If he started to follow too soon, his own dust trail would give him away immediately.

He lit a cigarette, took a deep drag and stared

down the dusty twin-rut trail. He should have taken them out in the mall parking lot while they were shopping. He'd done one like that once, in a crowd, and it was easy to just move off among the people afterwards. It was amazing how simple it was. It's just that with two of them you had to be more careful. Subcontrol hated mistakes.

Jesus, he thought, it's lonely out here.

She looked out the windows at the evening coming down. A massive cloud bank had risen to obscure the sunset, as it often did in the evening, only to disappear at dark, and the blackness had dropped like a thick blanket. She shivered. "It's so...so lonely."

He smiled. "Only if you don't understand it. We spend so much of our lives caught up in little constrained areas—apartments, houses, towns, cities—and when we have country open up around us, the way it does out here, it can be kind of scary at first. But if you look at it another way, it's all right."

"How's that?"

"Consider it a chance to open yourself up. Grow with the feeling rather than be frightened by it." He paused while he steered the truck down through a small gully and up around a caved-in bank. Something small and furry moved rapidly through the headlights.

"What was that?"

"Mouse. They flash like that in light because their belly fur is white."

"Where are we going to stop?"

"Another two miles, I think. Then you can set up camp and I'll try for some fish for dinner."

"In the dark?"

"By firelight. We'll be right next to the shore and the light draws them." He smiled. "Not too sporting, but pretty effective. We'll have a good dinner."

"Where are we going to sleep?"

"You're going to sleep in the back of the truck tonight. I'll sleep out away from the truck and the fire in a sleeping bag."

She coughed discreetly. "Look, I don't know how to say this, but don't you think in my case that modesty is a little silly?"

"Well, shucks, ma'am, no, I don't."

"That was an awful John Wayne."

"It was supposed to be Jimmy Stewart."

"It was a worse Stewart. Answer my question."

"Modesty has nothing to do with it." He got serious. "I'm just being cautious. Besides, in weather like this, when it's clear and summer warm, I like to sleep out on the ground."

"And I wouldn't?"

"Uhh, maybe not. Maybe for the first night you ought to stay inside. Just until you kind of get used to sleeping outside in the brush."

"What aren't you telling me?"

"Well, there are things, you know. Animals and things that might bother you a little if you're on the ground and aren't ready for them."

"Like what? What animals?"

"Coyotes will start singing towards morning and that can be a little scary. It sounds like a bunch of girls screaming. And then, of course," he dropped his voice to a husky whisper, "there's snakes."

"There's what?"

"Snakes," he said, louder. "Rattlesnakes."

"You're right. I'll sleep in the truck. Can the snakes get in the truck?"

"No. As a matter of fact they won't bother you on the ground, either. They're really not aggressive at all. But I wouldn't want you waking up in the middle of the night and seeing one and getting scared. You've been through enough."

"I agree." A bump slammed her against the door of the truck, and he slowed down and stopped. "What's the matter?"

"We're here."

She looked out the window and saw nothing but some rocks on the right and a grassy clearing on the left. All around were pines, though not terribly tall, and on the other side of the clearing she could see the black-slick shine of running water.

"It's beautiful," she said. "Like a fairy glade in books I used to read...."

"This is just our temporary camp," he said. "Wait'll you see where we're going to establish our base."

"Is it all right to get out?" She looked at the ground. "I mean, snakes and all?"

"Yeah. Damn, I shouldn't have even brought it up, about the snakes. Look, just relax. Almost nobody is killed by snakebite and you probably won't ever see one anyway. Just forget what I said, will you? The truth is that rattlesnakes are more afraid of you than you are of them."

"I doubt that." She shuddered. "But I'll work it out. What do we do first?"

"I'll get a fire going and get some trout. You

can make a bed area in the back of the truck and then change into those rough clothes. Don't forget the boots, they strengthen your ankles and keep you from getting rock bruised."

"Are they good for snakebite?"

"Oh, for Chrissakes. Forget that crap...." But he saw she was laughing and he smiled. "Yeah. They're good for snakebite."

He got out and left the lights on while he got a fire going in a small depression, then came back to the camper shell and got out the tube with the new rod and a bag with a reel and line. It took him five more minutes to get the reel set on the rod and the line through the eyelets and a small hook on the thin leader at the end. He took out a plastic worm and put it on the hook, and she watched it all with interest. She had changed clothes while he made the fire and looked clean and fresh, all creases and lines. Her blue denim work shirt still showed all the fold lines but they were losing fast to the richness of her body.

"Don't tell anybody I'm using plastic worms, right?" He smiled in the firelight—he'd turned the truck lights off to save the battery. "Very crude. No class at all. But trout won't rise to flies in the night and I'm hungry for some fresh fish."

"I have no idea what you're talking about." She leaned closer and looked at the worm. "It sure looks real. Is it plastic?"

"Yes." His voice dropped a full octave and he felt sweat come out on his upper lip. When she leaned forward the shirt opened and he found it hard not to stare. "Goddamn. You're beautiful, you know that? Even with the beating you took you're still a knockout."

"Yes. I know." She looked up, open and without artifice. "Would you like to go to bed with me?"

"Uhh...not like that. When and if it comes, all right. But not just like that, all right?"

"Sure. Whatever."

"I'll fish now, all right?"

"Sure. Whatever."

He turned for the stream but it took a full four steps before his mind started working again. He thought he'd never seen a woman so beautiful, so, so *woman*; she made a massive drive in him. It was something he did not understand and something that frightened him just a little because it was a part of his life he couldn't control.

The worm hit the water lightly, with a tiny flick, and almost immediately he had a trout on. Not big. Maybe ten inches. But it fought well and he had respect for the fish even though he felt cheap for using the worm.

In five minutes he had four nice trout. The light from the fire, a bright yellow beacon that the fish couldn't resist, pulled them almost into the bank.

He cleaned them on the bank, threw the guts back in the water and in four more minutes was frying the fish over the fire in cornmeal and butter.

She was humming while she worked in the back of the truck and John found himself smiling. It was a pleasant sound, on a pleasant night in beautiful country, and it was easy to imagine that none of that other crap was happening. Here there was just the light of the fire, and the summer-warm night and the stars and the fish smell coming off the pan and there were no computers, no Bixbys after them.

He let the serenity relax his neck and back muscles. They were safe, at least for the moment, and he needed the break from the running.

This time he swore viciously and with great venom and for an extended period of time, in a very professional manner.

The road was a Goddamn abomination, is what it was, and he was in a sedan trying to follow the truck without lights and with no moon. Disaster had been predictable, probably.

The sedan had low clearance, much lower than the little truck. He'd come down on a sharp rock after a bounce and the rock had punctured his oil pan. Of course he didn't know this at once, but found it after a time when the Goddamn oil light came Goddamn on, and he was Goddamn stranded in the middle of Goddamn nowhere on a Goddamn job he should have refused to take and to hell with the Goddamn consequences.

He tore the mobile phone off the bracket and called in.

Subcontrol was waiting. "You're four minutes late on your report time."

"Shit with that noise, I've got real problems out here."

"Swearing is not allowed over the net, you know that."

"Fuck you. My oil pan is gone and I'm out in the brush and I'm pissed off."

"Are you reporting a mission failure?"

"Goddamn it. . . ." He paused, thinking. If he reported a failure they would reissue the work to another operative and he would be forever suspect. Later they might make sure he never did it again. "Uhh. . .no. I just need some support."

"There is no support available in your present area in less than two days. Is there no way you can accomplish your mission yourself?" Subcontrol had a hangnail and he worked on it while he talked, surrounded by consoles and data decks. "We really must get this error rectified as soon as possible. Control has taken a personal interest."

It was, of course, a veiled threat. But it was well taken. Control had a way of making things unpleasant when he became personally involved. "I will have to continue on foot," he said. "Which means I won't be able to report at intervals."

"Affirmative. Report as you need to. Subcontrol out."

He slammed down the phone and sat fuming. It was a nearly hopeless situation and totally frustrating. His car was dead on a back road in the middle of the Goddamn mountains and his target was God knows how far ahead and he had to follow a car on foot.

"Son of a *bitch*."

And all because those two assholes in Denver couldn't get the job done. Damn. He reached beneath the car seat and took out the long-barreled .22 pistol he used for close-in work. It was a Ruger semiautomatic with a bull barrel to which he'd had weight added by a gunsmith so that there was absolutely no muzzle jump. It was like holding a hose. Initially he'd intended to make it all an accident, but that had changed. Now he'd have to correct the error any way he could.

Which was bullshit, of course, he thought, getting out of the car. Because it was entirely probable he would never see the subject again. He could be hundreds of different places, could be going many more miles. It was all very discouraging.

Then he caught the flicker of a yellow glow against the night sky.

It wasn't much. Just a yellow glow that kicked up softly off a rock and receded. Had he not been looking in exactly the right spot he would have missed it.

But he'd seen it. And as he watched the same place intently he saw it again, the same yellow puff of light, and he knew it was a fire, knew it was their fire, and he smiled.

It was off a fair distance, up above him somewhat, and he'd have to walk a long time to get there. But he knew where they were now, knew how to find them, was drawn to them the way the trout came to the light.

He started walking.

THIRTEEN

"That was delicious, absolutely wonderful." Barbara leaned away from the fire.

"It's true what people say—half the food you eat *does* taste better cooked over a fire. Or at least eaten next to a fire. *If* the chef is a master, like me." John smiled. "And if everybody is starving, dying of malnutrition."

"Stop talking. I want to enjoy myself."

He nodded, closed his mouth, smiled and leaned back. He could do dishes in a minute; it was enough now to just sit and enjoy the trout. It had been good at that, he thought. Not bad for somebody out of practice. "Where is it written that you can't just live like this?" John said suddenly. "I mean where is it written that we have to play all that other game crap? Why can't we just spend our days fishing and eating and hunting and sleeping and. . . ."

"Screwing," she said, lazily, stretching next to the fire. "I agree. To all of it. Except what happens when it snows?"

"We build a house."

"And where do we get the materials?"

"From a lumber yard. And we have to go to the bank for a loan to get the lumber and have to make payments to the bank. . ."

"I liked it better the other way," she said, rising. "I liked it when we just hunted and fished and screwed and. . . ."

"Would you really?" he asked, looking up.

She thought, rubbed the back of her neck. "No. But it sounds good, doesn't it?"

"Yeah."

She went off into the bushes, and he rose and went to the cab of the truck and took out the Sharps and the cartridges. He was sitting, cleaning it with an oily rag, when she came back.

"Do you really think it's necessary to have that out?"

"You saw how they came at us in the motel room, didn't you?" He said it hard, but then was embarrassed. He shrugged and smiled. "Hell, I'm sounding all melodramatic. I don't know. Frankly, I don't see how they could know where we are after we left Casper. They just couldn't be on us that fast. And yet. . . ."

"And yet what?" She moved back from the fire to get away from the heat.

"I don't know. Just a feeling. In Nam you always seemed to get hit the worst when you weren't expecting it. When you relaxed." He winced, remembering; whine-crack as they went close by your ear, thump when they went into meat, dull falling sound; noises, noises and every noise for killing, every noise from all things meaning a killing. "Or when you hunt. You go and go and your legs get tired and you start to get loose, get lazy, and that's when you get the shot, get the chance. We were very lucky back in the motel. We shouldn't have gotten away from them. I just don't want to use all my luck up—I thought if I got about half-ready it wouldn't hurt anything."

She looked at the flames. "I'm getting scared again."

"Don't be. I didn't mean to upset you." He put the rifle down and went around the fire and helped her to her feet. Then she was in his arms and he was holding her. "I don't think you have to be scared," he said, and realized how lame that sounded. "I mean, I'll try to protect you." That was worse, but it worked; she started giggling.

"God." She laughed openly, looking up into his face. "The macho role just doesn't work on you, does it?"

"No, I guess it doesn't." He was chuckling. "But Goddamn it, my heart is right. I mean those things."

"I know. I know." She folded into his arms again. "And I appreciate it. I really do."

The kiss was natural. It came. He was careful to kiss only the side of her mouth, because it was still bruised, and then they moved to the bed in the truck, because that was natural, too. They made love with a kind of earthy intensity that surprised both of them, so that when they moved together everything was right and when they were done, for a while, there was nothing else for them but their bodies and minds and the bed; there was none of the outside world.

The fire was dead. Even the embers had cooled. It was still dark but there was a faint lightness in the east, out across the great flats of the prairie which lay before him.

John sat up on a small rock outcropping just

above the fire area, about ten yards away from the truck in which Barbara was sleeping. He shivered with the morning cool that came down from the mountains. Even in midsummer the mountain nights were cool—some summers there was snow on the peaks all the way to fall.

He felt a bit like a fool, and he found himself smiling at himself as he sat up through the night. The love-making had absolutely wiped him, and here he sat on a Goddamn rock like some kind of just-pretend mountain man waiting for Indians.

It was ridiculous.

And yet twice, when he'd started to rise and go to the truck and sleep with her, which he wanted very much to do, something had stopped him, held him to the rock, and finally he'd just accepted it.

The night had gone slowly. They'd made love about eleven, and she'd slept afterward—was still sleeping. Now it was about four, and that meant he'd been sitting still and waiting for four and a half hours in the cold. But there had been beauty, the quiet beauty of the foothills, broken only by occasional song of coyotes. If he felt faintly foolish, he had also had plenty of time to think about a solution to their problem.

He hadn't come up with one yet, to be sure, but he'd been thinking of it all night—as soon as the glow of sex had worn off. His whole unlikely predicament still had him by the tail. It just didn't seem possible that a data man could be sitting at a console working a logic problem one day and find himself sitting guard with a buffalo gun in the mountains two days later, with a prostitute he'd half fallen in love with. It just couldn't happen.

And yet it had. And he was—as he'd been while in combat in Nam—terrified. He was being attacked by powerful forces he did not know, for reasons totally obscure to him. With indifference this Bixby was trying to eliminate him mentally and physically, as if he were a fly to be swatted. Why? Did it matter?

He had to act, forcibly. Sitting and thinking about it wouldn't save his neck, he was beginning to realize; as in a firefight the worst thing you could do was duck and hide. You had to attack. Otherwise, Bixby and his horde would just keep coming. . . .

A snapping sound stopped his thinking and his breathing at the same time. It hadn't been loud, just a tiny *crack* somewhere back down the road in the dark, but it had been a definite sound of intrusion, and John froze.

But heard nothing more. Only the thunder-rush of his blood pumping in his inner ear. No other sound.

Coyote? No. They moved too easily in the night to make a noise like that. It had been something heavier. Maybe a deer breaking a piece of dried cactus. Deer didn't move all that quietly, he reasoned. A buck moving through willows could sound like a bulldozer, busting and breaking.

A muffled *shuuff* this time. Not a deer, too soft. Maybe a bear, except that bear usually didn't work this low this time of the year, and if it were a bear there wouldn't be so much time from the crack to the shuffle because bear almost always kept moving.

He raised the barrel of the Sharps and eased

back the hammer, holding the trigger back until the hammer was at full cock so there wouldn't be a sound. He tried to push his vision across to where he'd heard the sound but he could see nothing, nor hear anything further. In the way of such things he began to doubt he'd heard anything in the first place. Then, next to a boulder on the side of the road, a shadow moved.

John stared just to the side of where he'd seen the shadow, letting his peripheral vision do the job of spotting movement in the pre-dawn light. He waited. The object moved again. It was a head.

Once he saw the head he saw the man, quite easily. Then he caught the flash of black-glisten off metal and knew that the man had a weapon. The man was there, moving in the night towards the truck; he had a gun in his hand, ready to kill with it.

All the talking that had been going on in John's head, the rationalizing, the macho poses, the *manana* vows, ceased. When they came to kill you, you killed them.

He brought the Sharps up and thought-felt the sight onto the center of the dark bulk, then lowered it a touch because of his tendency to shoot high at night. He pressed the rear set trigger, letting the click cut through the dark like a warning to freeze the target, to stop its movement for the shot.

He pressed the front hair trigger.

An immense flash and thunder filled the night. Sound and light roared out in a thirty-foot circle of burning powder, like a flashbulb only bigger and deafening beyond relief. In the flare of light he saw the bullet take the man.

The man went into a macabre dance. The huge slug bent him in the middle and doubled him backwards along the ground, his writhing outlined in the yellowed explosion of the black powder. There was a distinct whistle of air from his nostrils. Then the light died. John dropped the lever and put another cartridge in the rifle, just in case. And that was when the high-pitched screams started.

"*Neeeeeeeeeeeeaahhhh! Neeeeeeeeaaah!*"

They were, quite literally, screams so full of horror that they all but stopped the listener's heart. John had heard them before, from gut-shot men in Nam who'd been torn in half and died the way this man was dying. But Barbara, who'd been awakened in the truck by the explosion, had never heard them. She came bolting from the truck, running out and away from the unbelievable screeches until he ran after her, stopped her and held her.

"My God!" she cried in his ear. "What is it? Make it stop. I can't stand it. Turn it off, turn it off!"

He grimly turned her head away, then raised the rifle again. But even as he did so the pitch of the screams became lower and, in seconds, were muted. The only sounds were short pantings.

"Son of a bitch," John muttered. "Die and be done."

She saw his narrowed eyes and face cold with fury then, in the morning light, and these chilled her almost as much as the screaming had. She saw that John was a killer, that both of them had been wrong earlier in thinking he wasn't, that there was something savage in him beyond her tampering with.

"Stay here," he said, and went over to the man on the ground. He lay curled in a ball holding what used to be his middle, some dark pasty substance in the half light.

"You work for Bixby?" John asked him.

But the man didn't see him, didn't hear the question. He knew only his bright core of pain and his sense of his life draining out. It would soon be done. There would be no more sun, no more food, no more sex and no more breathing. He finally gasped the right word:

"Fuck."

He died, wet and messed twitching. John turned away because that part, the ending, was private even for those you hated. He walked up the hill and sat on a rock with the rifle across his lap and was brooding that way when she came over to him.

"He was here to...kill us?"

"That's right," John said briefly. Then, "You know what? Shit! Just shit!"

Suddenly, to her surprise, he was crying, staring at the body and just crying. At first, she did not understand. Then she began to sense that he was torn by something from the war he'd been in; something that encompassed killings in general, not just this one, and that he had death and slaughter horrifically on his mind. She took him in her arms and rocked him until his crying receded to sobs. Finally, he began breathing normally and regained some control.

He stood then. There was enough light now to see well by. He went back to the body once more, this time to look for some kind of identification on it. But when he turned the body on its stomach and saw the exit wound, he changed his mind. The man's spilled-out intestines had obliterated his wallet and most everything else, including the label on his pants.

He shook his head in despair. What difference did it make? He walked back to where Barbara sat. "I don't know who he is, but we'll have to leave anyway. They know where we are or he wouldn't have been here. Let's get packed up."

"Where did he come from?" She sat still, studiously avoiding looking in the direction of the body.

"Up the road. In the dark. He must have parked way back somewhere and walked because I didn't hear an engine."

"Tell me. . .the truth. . .did you have to kill him like that?"

John looked into her eyes for a long time. Something inside her was shaking. "No. I could have let him kill you. I did what I thought was best."

She closed her eyes. Opened them. "You're different," she said. "You've changed."

"Maybe it's not me that's changed so much as your way of seeing me."

"Maybe. Maybe we're both right. I'll think about it some more." Despite her horror at what he'd done, she managed a smile at him.

After that she got up and in silence helped load their things in the back of the truck. They climbed in then, but John stopped before he turned the key.

"Where are we going?" she said quietly.

"Just wondering that myself. I was thinking

of burying the body before we leave. Only one kind of gun can make a wound like that—my buffalo gun—and if they find the body they'll know I did it."

She shook her head. "They're going to know that sooner or later anyway, aren't they? I've got a better idea. Let's go find the car he came in. It can't be far. You said he came from the east?"

She looked at him until some of the aggressiveness she'd discovered in him came back into his eyes. "Yeah," he breathed. "Damn good idea."

They drove east back over the gravel road. When they'd gone three miles, perhaps a bit more, they came upon the car jammed over to the side of the ruts. Oil stained the ground beneath it. John stopped the truck, got out cautiously, and looked the car over.

"Blew his pan on a rock," he called back to Barbara. "And there's a phone in the car. It's just as we thought. He was reporting back and they know exactly where we are. Christ," he swore almost in admiration, "what an organization."

He got into the truck again and drove faster now. After they'd gone half the distance to the freeway—both riding in silence—he rubbed his face to get rid of the tired feeling, then the back of his neck. "Wow, sitting on a rock all night—I'm too old for that crap," he said. "On the other hand, what if I hadn't sat there?"

Still she said nothing, and he turned to her. "What's the matter now? You're supposed to be the cheerer-upper."

"Now it's me that's down," she said. "It all

just hit me—all of it. And now that phone in the car...." She looked morose. "I mean these people are really big, John. Bixby can find us and kill us no matter what we do. We don't have a Goddamn chance. Not a one."

He said nothing for a moment, then reached a hand out to touch hers. "It's not hopeless."

"The hell it isn't. You can't just sit on a hill like something out of a western movie and blow them away with that buffalo gun. They'll get you sooner or later. And I hate to tell you this, sport, but you don't seem to know what else to do. Right now, you're a chicken roaming around without a head. And Jesus Christ, I'm flapping my wings right alongside you!"

Even knowing that she was saying cruel things out of her own despair, he bristled. "The hell you say. What do you know about it? The fact is I've come up with some angles we can work."

"For example?" she shot at him.

"For example—" he found himself rising to the occasion"—Bixby either runs or is high up in an organization of huge size and efficiency."

"Runs," she said, nodding. "Bet on it—there's nobody over him. So?"

"So. So the bigger an organization, the easier it is to fight it, that's what. Guerilla gangs have known that for a long time—stay small, move fast, and you can beat an army. But I've got more than that. Listen to me. The one thing we know for certain is that Bixby's doing something illegal—and something very big."

"So he's Mafia?" She bounced as he heedlessly drove the truck over a rock. "It could be, I suppose."

"No, I don't think Mafia." John shook his

head. "I think it's something else, something bigger."

"*Bigger* than the Mafia?"

"Yeah. I think...wait a minute, we're coming up on the freeway." In the near distance there were cars and trucks wheeling by, none of them obeying the 55-mph limit. John stopped before the overpass and thought for a moment. "Which way? That's the question."

"You're asking me?" she said. "Big shot is asking me?"

He glowered at her. "I'm asking myself. I've got a plan but I don't think it matters too much whether we go north or south to carry it out."

She looked at him doubtfully. "You've got a plan? You really have?"

"Yeah. It just hit me while we were talking. We're going to bust that son of a bitch wide open and he won't even know we're doing it."

"We are?"

He nodded. He didn't answer in words, but she knew from the new set of his head that he had something substantial going for him. It was infectious, and she found herself feeling optimistic for absolutely no other reason she could discern than his confidence.

John looked at the fuel gauge. "We'll go north. We've still got three-quarters. I guess we can make it to where we're going even if the stations are closed."

"Where are we going?" She watched him accelerate, spin the wheel and zoom onto the freeway. "You might keep me informed—I am half of this mess, you know."

"Sorry. I was just getting wrapped up in the details of it." He settled into the left speed lane.

"We have to find a computer terminal where we won't be bothered. The one reason I have for going north is that I know a man up here with a small computer terminal he uses for business—it's a mail-order setup. It will work well enough for our purpose if we can get to use it."

"What are we going to do?"

"We're going to go inside Bixby's Goddamn operation and take it over without his knowing about it. If I'm right, he's doing the biggest computer ripoff in history. He may be taking over the country, if not the world, through economic means."

"Oh, come on." She shook her head. "I'll buy a lot about the bastard but I can't go that far."

"No. It can happen. I used to sit and think about it, about ways you could do it, and I often wondered if anybody would ever try it. There have been big computer crimes—for example, in Texas a whole oil corporation was taken over by one man using a computer hook-in. He bled them down until they went bankrupt and they never knew he was doing it. He got them for over two hundred million dollars, wiped them out, and would have gotten completely away with it except that his wife found out he was doing it and turned him in."

"Low blow."

"They had filed and she was pissed." John smiled. "Another example of happy marriage."

"But a whole country?"

"Yeah. I think so. I don't know, but it could happen. That's what we're going to find out, if I can get the use of this guy's terminal. He owes me a favor from Nam, kind of. Well, not owes me, but I think he'll help."

"What did you do for him?"

"Nothing really. Just work, you know, just what comes up when the shit's down—work. I pulled him back by the ankles and he thinks I saved his life. But he would have done the same for me. Did, as a matter of fact. Several times."

He fit in behind a truck to get the pull, automatically saving gas, and smiled. "His name is Carl Jackson and he used to say he didn't give a shit for nobody nohow but I don't think that's quite true. At least I hope not, because we need a pile of help from him."

He sat quietly driving into the warm morning, remembering things about Carl Jackson from another time.

FOURTEEN

Carl Jackson was a huge bear of a black man with a smile, when he smiled, that was wide and genuine. He gave such a smile now to an old Nam buddy.

"Goddamn it, Smith, it is *good* to see you!" he boomed. He'd driven his jeep down and met the truck in the driveway entrance, down by the mailbox, and took John out and held him up in the air—literally—to look him over. "Soft living didn't seem to ruin you. You're looking fine."

"A little soft," John wheezed, "like in my ribs. You're breaking them."

Jackson laughed and put John down. Then he looked in the truck to where Barbara still sat. "You sure found a pretty woman, but why have you been beatin' her?"

"I haven't. And she's not my woman. Not really." John reached out and turned Carl around. "Listen Carl, before we go any further, I've got to tell you something. I'm in a world of shit, man, a really bad one. And I need help. It's serious, really straight."

Carl's smile drew down. "Hell, man, it can't be worse than the shit we took down on us in Nam, can it?"

John looked at him, then nodded slowly. "It's

been running that way, friend. I left meat back down in Wyoming." John dropped into Nam jargon easily. "There's a bad guy looking for my ass—our ass," he gestured back to Barbara in the truck, "and he will waste our ass if he finds us. Straight."

Carl let his glance slip to Barbara and back to John. "Is it law?"

"No. It isn't the law. It's the other way."

"Mafia?"

"No. I don't think so—maybe." John sighed. "Look, I'm telling you all this in front because we're friends and I don't want you to get involved without knowing what's going down. This is just one heavy son of a bitch and it could be dangerous. You got a family yet?"

"No. A woman named Bev lives with me and we get along well, but no kids. Let me ask you something and we'll get down to drinking: can this son of a bitch you're talking about be whipped?"

John thought of the times in Nam when he'd felt neither of them could possibly have lived; of the quick-screams of the hit and dying; of the hot air alive with buzzes and pops. They'd survived the menace and the bullets too—with all their faculties intact, or almost. He looked at the Montana evening through the pines bordering Carl's driveway and he nodded. "Yes. I think he can. But I need help."

"Then you got it. Now bring your woman and we'll get to the house and I'll show you how the idle rich live."

"She's not my woman and I didn't know you were rich."

"I'm not." Carl called over his shoulder. "I

just live like they do."

John jumped into the truck and followed Carl up the driveway.

"He's black," Barbara said, having sat quietly in the cab throughout the whole greeting.

"You noticed," John said, smiling. "Why, does it bother you?"

"Not in the least. I just thought it might bother you."

"*Me*? Why?"

"Because...because you're so straight. You just seem to be so Waspy, so straight."

John laughed. "Hell, everybody is straight with some people. You relax with a buddy. You'll have to quit projecting. It never works."

"Yes. I guess I'll do that."

The driveway was two-and-a-half miles long and led back into the low rock mountains north of Deborgia, Montana. It was like driving through sequential scenes in a nature calendar; crag bluffs hanging over rippling trout streams, thick clumps of green pines, beaver ponds lying like jewels in the road-bordering waterway. The road was well-maintained and they made good time to the house.

Carl's place was pioneer American in style. In a large clearing, he'd built an immense two-story log house, with roof dormers and a long slant-roof room on the south side. All the logs had been peeled and varnished and shone in the evening light. It had been a long day's drive and Barbara was tired, but she still sat up. "My God, it's beautiful."

John nodded. "When we got out of Nam I went into data and Carl came up here. He had a relative in the south who died and left him a chunk of money when we were over in the shit. It was enough to buy a few hundred acres. He got a chain saw and came in and built this house."

"Alone?"

John nodded. "There was a time then when we all wanted to be alone. He was just going to stay back in here and say to hell with it, come out once a spring maybe, but the money started to fade so he started a mail-order business."

"What does he sell?"

"Possibles."

"Why not probables?"

He laughed. "Possibles is a term for geegaws, stuff the old mountain men used, parts for old rifles, kits for leather clothes, stuff like that."

"And he makes a living off it?"

"He doesn't get rich. But he seems to be doing all right, doesn't he?"

She nodded and was going to say more when a pack of dogs—a dozen or so—came barreling around the side of the building and started yipping and jumping up at the truck, tails wagging furiously. The din they set up stopped all further conversation.

John decided to throw caution to the winds and get out. Instantly, the dogs were all over him, leaping up and licking him. He almost went over backwards before Carl came back from parking his jeep and pulled them off.

"*Get* down, Goddamn it. Come on, Eustace, Goddamn it Enrique, get your asses *down*." He pulled John upright. "Sorry. They don't see many people and like to get acquainted fast."

The house's front door had opened at the

noise, and a handsome woman was standing there, grinning sympathetically at the jam John had been in. He glanced at her, then brushed himself off, getting ready to meet her. She had long black hair down to her waist, which was slim, and she came forward to greet him with the grace and vitality of a young girl. As she got closer, John could see from certain wrinkles around her eyes that she was probably into her late thirties.

"Bev," Carl said, smiling, "I'd like you to meet my good friend John and his woman Barbara."

"She's not my wo...oh, to hell with it." John turned back to the truck. "Come out, Barbara, the dogs are friendly." Wheeling back to Bev he widened his smile. "I'm very glad to meet you, Bev."

"Come on in. There's coffee on the stove." She took his hand. Barbara got out of the truck and waded around through the dogs. When she came alongside John, Bev looked over to her and something went on between them; John caught the look, a moment during which their eyes met and everything about both of them seemed known by the other. But exactly what had transpired between them he had no way of knowing; he made a mental note to ask Barbara about it later.

Inside the house was cool, quiet, as one would expect from its calm, early American exterior. The wide-board pine floor of the living room was oiled and covered with Indian rugs, and there were more such rugs hanging on the walls. A massive white quartz fireplace dominated this room. To the left was the kitchen, with a huge wood stove for cooking and a hand pump at the sink. And down one step on the right was Carl's warehouse and office, with his merchandise for sale identical in feel to the furnishings of his house. There were Indian wall-hangings in this room too, along with bows, arrows, powder horns, leather clothing, flint and percussion rifles. Some of the things were old, some new. All around the base of the walls were metal pull-out bins, containing the rest of Carl's large stock. There were dozens of them.

"You're looking plenty substantial," John said, taking it all in.

Carl explained, "There's this mini-boom going on in this stuff." He laughed. "Hell, I never wanted to get rich, only to enjoy myself. Now I'm probably going to get rich anyway—ain't that the luck of it?"

"Ain't it?"

"Remember how nobody used to want to hootch with me because I had no luck?" Carl said. "And you did?"

"Because I was dumb."

"And we're the only two made it through all that shit."

"Yeah."

They were silent for a time, with the two women standing awkwardly next to them. Finally, Bev broke the long quiet. "Barbara, I'll bet you want to clean up after all day in the truck. Why don't you come with me and I'll show you the facilities."

"I was curious," Barbara said, nodding. "I saw the hand pump on the kitchen sink...."

"No—we've got hot and cold running water.

The pump is for backup if the main system freezes."

"Does that happen often?"

"In the winter," Bev said, with something close to reverence in her voice, "*everything* freezes."

Carl and John watched the two women leave. "She seems nice," John said, gesturing with his chin towards Bev. "More than you deserve."

"Shit." Carl said, laughing, then his voice got quiet and serious. "Truth is, friend, I was going to ask her to marry me. We do get along, you know? I just love hell out of her."

John slammed him on the back. "I'm happy for you. Really. I wish it all good for you."

"Thanks." Carl shrugged. "But this ain't getting it done for you, is it? What do you need first?"

"Your computer terminal—do you still have that one with a printout on it?"

"Better. When things got hot with my business I got a bigger model with a screen."

"Fantastic!"

"Yeah. Now I don't have to poop around with paper, for one thing. And I've got an automatic linkup with my suppliers if I gotta back order something. It's just slicker than hell...Well, what the hell, listen to me telling a computer man what computers are all about. Christ."

John looked around. "Where is it?"

"Back with the storage bins—you can't see it from here. Come on, I'll show you."

John followed him into his office and saw the computer terminal on a desk. It had a small viewing screen and a small typewriter style keyboard—in fact it looked like a much-miniaturized version of the console he'd worked on back in Denver.

Back in Denver! Christ, when was that!

"What's the matter, man? You look like your brain stopped."

John shook his head. "I guess it did. I was just trying to figure out how long it's been since all this happy horseshit started. I think it's only three or four days but it seems like a month."

"You gonna tell me about it? About this heavy son of a bitch you gotta fight?"

John pulled the chair out from the desk and sat. "Yeah, I'll tell you. Everything I know, at any rate."

He made it brief. Everything he knew, from the initial hassle with the Shoshone bank cashier to using the fifty-ninety on the man in Wyoming. He told it as straight as he could except that he glossed over the relationship between Bixby and Barbara—he didn't say that Barbara had been, correction, *was* a hooker, only that she had been involved with Bixby and had called to save John's life.

"So what have I got?" he asked Carl, when he'd finished.

Carl frowned. "Hell, *I* don't know. Isn't there something you can guess about? Some ideas you've got? If that man is playing with eighty-two million, and it's real money and not just a mistake, then he must be doing something really wrong—nobody makes that kind of money doing it right."

"Yeah. I know."

"So you got an idea?"

"Yeah." John stared at the computer terminal and licked his lips.

"What is it?"

"I'm not sure it will work. I think this Bixby is into computer crime on a scale that makes all previous computer crime a joke. I thought I could come up here and use your computer terminal and my kludge box to find out what's going on and stop the son of a bitch. But now I don't know. . . ."

"Why?"

"Don't know what?" Bev came into the room. "I left Barbara in the tub with bubbles and steam." She shook her head. "There isn't an inch where she hasn't been hit. Somebody sure worked her over—was it you?" She looked squarely into John's eyes.

"No. It was the man I was talking about when you came in."

"Good." Bev nodded. "My grandfather used to think a woman needed a beating now and then, but I don't. I'm glad it wasn't you." There was fire in her eye but it receded as she spoke. "I would have kicked you out."

"She would have, too," Carl added, without smiling. "She can be hard, man, really hard."

"So what about this guy?" Bev asked.

John repeated the story. "The problem is that if I'm right, I almost can't be right."

"That makes it all clear to me," Bev said, laughing. Carl joined her. "I was worried that I wouldn't understand. . .now I know I won't."

"No. Listen. If this Bixby is in computer crime, fine—even if he's really got a huge operation going, that's still something I can handle. But my God, he's got people all over—he's got a Goddamn army out there, right? And apparently computer links all over the country. To support that kind of a setup he's got to be almost a government unto himself. He's into everything...and I'm not sure we can stop him."

"But you've got to try, right?" Carl said, smiling. "You haven't got any choice, way I see it. Either you cut this bastard's head off or he'll kill you. He's not letting you make the decisions."

John rubbed the back of his neck and closed his eyes and opened them slowly. "Yeah. I know you're right—knew that was what had to be all along. I just didn't want to admit it. It's a hell of a box, isn't it?"

Carl didn't answer.

"Yeah. Well, I'll need to set up a program to ask the right questions," John said, looking back at the terminal. "That's a toughie and I'm tired. I'll sleep on it and get into it tomorrow morning. Then we shall see what we shall see...."

FIFTEEN

The coyote was a keen, intelligent hunter. It came from a goodly distance off in response to the odor of hot, sun-baked meat.

When it was five yards from the meat it circled around it, whining, looking for signs of a trap, since it was man-meat and that meant that other men, moving ones, might be nearby to do him harm. Finally the coyote stood over the meat, legs tensed, ready to flee.

Still no movement. The coyote put its nose down, smelled the most odorous part and was about to lap, to obey its instinct to gorge when the sound came.

Engine. Far off yet but coming steadily, the rough cough of power the coyote knew from pickups and jeeps. It moved from the body, letting the flies have it, and ran off up the foothills. Engines were death. The coyote ran zigzag, cutting from gully to rock, until it was well away from the body by the stream. Then it settled down into a bouncing mouse-hunting pattern that would have its belly full in thirty minutes. There was plenty of other good meat in the area.

Two men got out of the jeep and walked over

to the body. One turned away, but the other had been at Khe Sahn where they'd taken eighteen hundred rounds a day and there was nothing but bodies like this.

"Christ, what did he get hit with—a cannon?" he asked with professional interest. "There's almost two of him."

"Shit, Harve, don't talk like that," the other said nervously, still with his back to the body.

Harve gave no indication of hearing his partner. He turned the lower half of the body with his foot and reached down with two fingers to remove the gut-smeared wallet from the back pocket. "Seems to be the only identification on him. On the way back down we'll check the car. It was rented so there are probably no links in it. Just this wallet. That ought to make control happy."

The other one still did not turn. "Shouldn't we bury him or something?"

Harve let the body flop back over. "We'll do the 'or something.' We'll leave him for the buzzards."

He moved back to the jeep, took the mobile phone from the rack and got patched into subcontrol.

"Nobody here but your operative and he's decommissioned," he said. "The situation is as you predicted. The mission failed." He was careful not to get too specific over the mobile phone. "What now?"

"You're making sure there are no links with us?"

"Affirmative. Suggest we leave immediately."

There was a pause.

"That's affirmative. Go to Casper and await

further instructions. We're going to run a cross-match program on the subject's known associates in that area. The airline computers don't show him leaving it, at any rate. You may be called in to correct the error. Check in at any motel chain and we'll find you when we need you."

"Roger."

Harve and his partner got in the jeep and drove off back down the gravel road toward the freeway. Harve, despite his outwardly cool demeanor, was worried. He was still, effectively, in training—had joined the organization only seven months before and wasn't that certain about his future in it. He was no longer certain, that is, that he wanted to be part of it, now that he had seen some of the job's ramifications close up. For all his combat experience, he had trouble forgetting the way the operative on the ground had looked where the fifty-caliber bullet had gone through him.

He wondered if he could resign.

Far behind the departing jeep, the coyote took its time and went back to the body.

SIXTEEN

John stared at the blue-white glow on the screen, hands poised on the keyboard, thinking.

It was three twenty-six in the morning. Everybody else was still asleep. He was alone, put a pot of coffee on the wood stove and, while waiting for it to brew, had once more reviewed the tricky aspects of his undertaking.

The problem was to get inside Bixby's setup without Bixby knowing about it. And then to destroy it.

Simple.

But almost impossible to accomplish. Except that he was going to give it a whirl anyway.

He'd come to the console with his coffee and carefully tied his kludge box into the telephone line hooked to Carl's terminal. That part was easy. He smiled while he worked, as he always smiled—a bit grimly—when he thought of how easily the telephone system could be linked into computers.

It was paradoxical that people still worried about telephone privacy, fearing they might be bugged or otherwise have their lives interfered with; they'd gone to great lengths to have laws against wire tapping passed—in most states a court order was required to wiretap.

And yet the worst damage had been done without their knowledge. Quietly, over a ten or fifteen year period, computers had been linked with existing telephone systems throughout the entire country. Privacy was no longer possible. Any computer could be inserted almost instantly between anybody's phone and any other computer in the world. While all the conversations in the world were going on, the same wires and microwave systems could be used to transport selected data of any desired kind.

The power of the computer network had become positively awesome, John mused as he worked. Often he'd visualized its current and theoretical capabilities. Think of it. If you got stopped for a traffic ticket now and the cop read your license number into his mobile phone, he was automatically linked into all the criminal computer systems in the world, and if you were wanted for a crime anywhere, he'd have that knowledge instantly and could arrest you on the spot. That maybe was increased efficiency in a good cause. But it was the least of it. In hundreds of subtle ways, computer-phone systems had moved in to wipe out people's jobs and so wreck their lives, all in the name of efficiency. A grocery store owner in northern Minnesota, for example, notices that he's low on certain items. He carries a hand-held computer terminal tape system down his aisles and runs a light-sensitive wand over little strips of dark lines on the shelves. These are his product identification strips. Then he goes to the phone, dials the correct number for his computer link, plays the tape into the phone and hangs up.

Instantly, his product shortages are fed into the main computer in Dallas. One product shortage is shunted to a computer in Italy to make sure the product hasn't seen a new price increase at its source, then sent back with the other automatic requests to a supply computer in Fargo, North Dakota. There a printout jerks out the information that on the next shipment the grocery store is to receive, along with the rest of its order, an extra case of imported olives.

All of this in less then a second—without clerks, salesmen, bookkeepers, secretaries or any of the other people needed formerly to run the system. Efficient, but devastating to whole areas of human life.

There was nothing to be done about it, John thought. Short of pulling all the plugs on all the data banks, or forcibly erasing all the memory systems and starting over, human privacy and any reasonable sort of human job security were at an end.

John took a sip of the coffee. He let his mind slip a bit more and wondered how many cups of similar coffee he'd had in his career in data systems. Always the coffee, and the whine of equipment and the printout sheet or glowing screen.

Almost four in the morning now.

Almost six in New York, nearly five in Los Angeles—different times wherever Bixby's net reached. How to break into it? What was the program? How to pop inside Bixby's organization and wreck it without his knowledge?

He had to control his hatred of Bixby, at least distance himself from his feelings long enough to work out what was essentially a problem in data handling. The program he chose depended on what the other side was up to.

The first step was to think about data-oriented crime in general—what the F.B.I. had chosen to call computer crime. With billions of dollars and tons of material—everything from cars to building supplies—being shuffled around the world, it hadn't taken long for a percentage of the data handlers to realize they were onto a good thing.

Computer crime had started small, with a few thousand dollars lifted here and there which nobody missed. But in a very short time the pilfering took on staggering proportions. The amount of money gathered in through data stealing couldn't actually be measured because the stealing didn't always really happen. It just appeared to happen. A data criminal could electronically lift money from an account in a bank, deposit it in his own bank at the other end of the country, use it to establish a line of credit or get a huge loan, then electronically put the money back in the account he'd taken it from and erase the entire event so that it never happened.

He could do this over his telephone with a kludge box—like the one John himself had built—a small tonal oscillator that could be made from shelf items. And all without leaving his living room. Effectively, he had a computer terminal, like Carl Jackson's—or the Shoshone bank's for that matter.

Another classic form of data-oriented skulduggery had the perpetrator continually shifting money from one account in a given bank and then keeping this electronic shuffleboard going from one bank to the next so that a shortage never appeared. You had to know bank codes, but for somebody who worked in data they weren't hard to learn. If you dealt in millions you could become a very rich man in a very short time. Hundreds of millions were being moved illegally that way all the time. It was the perfect crime because once the benefit had been derived from it, it could be made electronically never to have happened! The F.B.I. was so concerned about computer crime that it had organized a whole new section just to combat it. But the worrisome question remained; how do you fight a crime when all the evidence shows that it never took place?

And John knew of two types of computer crime even more sophisticated than those two. Nonexistent companies had been fabricated electronically, for example. When these "companies" did business with real companies, all the transactions were handled electronically, via the criminal's computer terminal. He could order millions of dollars worth of goods delivered to an empty lot (this had actually happened several times) and then electronically "pay" the bill. The selling company would find itself millions of dollars short without having any evidence pointing to fraud. A man could buy anything that way, never pay for it, yet always seem to have paid for it. There was nothing that couldn't be had—you could get anything.

A computer terminal? Hell, John thought, you could get a big-daddy computer itself!

His pulse quickened and he sat up straight at Carl's terminal console. That was it! If a crook with a terminal ran a shifting operation, he could get rich. If he had a second terminal and set up a phony company he could get doubly rich. But two terminals were about all a man could handle without losing track of what was going on—working alone, that is.

But if the man owned a *computer*, the whole thing, and programmed it to handle not only money shifting and/or any limited number of specific frauds—but programmed it to function on the more abstract level of Crime itself, Crime with the capital C. . . .

"My God," John almost shouted. "That's it—that's what he's doing. He's using a Goddamn computer to commit computer crime!"

"What did you say?"

The voice startled him and he turned to see Barbara standing in the entryway behind him.

"What are you doing up?"

"I turned over and you weren't there and I got worried." She was wearing a thin wrap-around summer robe she'd gotten from Bev. It did absolutely nothing to hide the lushness of her body. Her hair fell down around her face in an unplanned but lovely manner and the effects of her beating were almost gone. Along with his joy at having, possibly, fathomed Bixby's scheme, John felt a passion for her rise in him.

"You look beautiful," he said softly, and wondered at the secondary feeling of warmth—a little tug of something he didn't expect in the back of his mind. Fondness. No, more than that. "You look truly beautiful."

She blushed. "Thank you." She looked directly into his eyes then for several beats, and something passed between them; something that neither of them completely understood but knew could grow if they let it.

"There's coffee on the stove," he said quietly. "Can I get you some?"

"I'll get it."

She left and went to the darkened kitchen and he heard her find a cup and fill it and walk back. "How is it going?" she asked, sitting on one of the boxes near him.

"I think I'm onto something," he said. He told her briefly of his reasons for believing Bixby might have decided to use a major computer to commit crime.

She said wonderingly, "Could he do that?" She took a sip of coffee. "Aren't there safeguards that would make something like that impossible?"

"No. Yes. I mean, there are safeguards, blocks built into all systems, and they're supposed to work. But those safeties are put in by people, and if people can put them in people can break them. That's always been the one big worrisome aspect of the world's computer economy, that one crooked person who knew all the safeties could blow the whole thing wide open. The system has been living simply on the hope that it would never happen...."

"And now it has happened," she said. "Bixby is the one."

"Yes. I think Bixby has programmed a computer to commit crimes against other computers; to get inside their systems and transfer funds, take over companies, start and stop fraudulent new companies, take it all." He took a breath. "He could take it *all*—the whole

Goddamn works. He could run the world."

"Oh, John, really! I mean, I agree that he's powerful but taking over the world...."

"No, really, listen." His eyes were intense, and she immediately got caught up in his thinking. "There's no limit to what he can do if he has an entire computer geared into crime—no limit. For instance, if he wanted to do a simple fraudulent transfer—say, lift five thousand from a corporate account and put it in a secret account and then cover the fact that it's gone, if he wanted to do that he could just program one section of the computer to commit that particular type of crime. Making contact with banking computers, breaking their codes, ruffling through their accounts to see which is the most vulnerable at the moment, taking the money and covering the evidence of its disappearance—all of it could be done, essentially, by pushing a button. The computer does it all. It's truly automated crime."

"I see that. But that's only five thousand dollars—it's not exactly taking over the whole world's economy."

"Yeah. I know. But if he's got a decent system going he can do say five or six thousand transfers an hour—assuming he's locked into foreign banks as well—around the clock, and only use one small section of his computer to do it."

"Five thousand times an hour? But that's, that's..."

"Like I said—that's all of it. And that's only one function possible with his system. He could be doing other forms of company raiding, material transfer, land transfers, phony fund moving, fake credit lines—all of it. He could be doing all of it at once, doing it all the time. And by locking his system into police computer systems he could tell up front what suspicious activity they were investigating, if any. God! They'd never catch him because they'd be using computers to do it and his computer would be running one jump ahead of theirs, wiping things clean just ahead of where they were looking. Nobody could touch him. Nobody could even come close to him."

"Except you."

"Except us," John corrected. "We saw a mistake and you. . .got involved with Bixby. All a matter of bad luck. If that hadn't happened at the same moment so you could warn me, Bixby would have just gone on with it. Now we can stop him."

"How?"

"That. . .ahh, that is a good question. I'm not sure. There are two ways open to us—first, we can call the F.B.I. computer crime section and tell them what Bixby is doing. Except you know what happened the last time we called the cops."

"Bixby knew where we were."

"Right. The second thing we can do is steal Bixby's computer. Steal the whole Goddamn thing from him without his knowing we're doing it."

"Can we do that?"

"We can try." John said, nodding, turning back to the console of Carl's terminal. "We can give it one hell of a try."

There was excitement in his voice and Barbara noticed it and wondered when she'd heard it before. Then she remembered. His voice had sounded the same way just after he'd shot the man in the mountains and was waiting for him to die. The same excitement and almost uncontrolled anger.

She was frightened by his anger. But exhilarated by it too.

SEVENTEEN

It was an incredibly tedious job. The data operator had to cross-feed all of John Smith's known associates back through their IRS Form 1040's, their FICA accounts, credit card accounts, motor vehicle registrations, *et cetera*.

His neck and shoulders ached from the time-consuming boredom of it. He was sick of drinking coffee. He wanted to go home and screw the socks off his wife and then forget all about computers and data for at least a week and a half.

But control had an intense personal interest in this one that had filtered all the way down to the operator level. He'd been given a detailed program to follow and he wasn't to curtail it until John Smith's current whereabouts were pinpointed.

He had this ridiculous list of Smith's army buddies, another of his work associates over the years, another of his known women. He had to check each of them to see which had current addresses in a five-state area around Colorado and which of those had connections with Smith close enough, in any of a number of ways, to indicate a probability of their harboring him. The degree of probability had to be ascertained.

He had to pipe the information back to Denver after finding out all he could about these people that might aid in error rectification for a Goddamn diode that had blown and let data out and he wasn't even in charge of the section of the computer where the Goddamn diode had Goddamn blown.

The data operator gritted his teeth. Army buddies. Might as well start there. Smith had been a noncom in the Seventh Cavalry in Vietnam. He locked into the military data link, worked back through regimental records and found him in the first platoon of Company C. He got the platoon's full roster, along with the stateside addresses of the men, and stored them. Though many would have moved by now, it was a place to start. . . .

It looked like a Goddamn nightmare of soft data. But, if he didn't come up with something, hand control was going to land on his head. He started scanning the names.

Wesley R. Novotny. Wartime address: Yankton, South Dakota.

He ran the name back through the income tax system and found that Novotny was living currently in St. Louis. That ruled him out.

William S. Craig, Louisville, Kentucky. Deceased. Car wreck.

Peter Echels, Tulsa, Oklahoma. . . .

It was going to be a long search and the data operator felt his acid rise into heartburn. Goddamn.

John got inside the Denver Data Center. Of course that was the easy part—he knew all the regular codes, all the program formats, and he had one stroke of luck; not figuring on his going after their systems, they had changed nothing in the four days since he'd worked there.

Fingers resting on the keyboard, he let out a long breath. "That's step one," he said to Barbara.

She looked at the screen, saw only numbers. "That's it? It's that easy?"

"If you know the codes," he nodded. "Just like that."

"What good does it do us?"

"It all depends on what you want to do. We can rifle accounts, move money around, wipe out accounts or take everything they own...."

"But all you did was push a few buttons and make some numbers appear on the screen. You didn't *do* anything."

"That's all you ever do. That's all the whole system does, remember? It's just moving numbers around and pushing buttons. That's all Bixby does, and look where he is."

She looked at the terminal and at John and after a moment she laughed, nervously. "It's all so silly, isn't it? None of it means anything to anybody. It's like a little numbers game, where all you can win is more numbers."

He nodded and said, with a tight smile, "I agree. There's no sense to it. Still, we've got to play the game because if we don't Bixby is going to kill us. *He's* making it mean something, even if we're not."

She quit laughing. "You're right, of course. What do we do next?"

John looked out the window. A spectacular sunrise, the kind only the west can provide, was kicking up huge sweeps of color, a splattering of reds and pinks radiating in garish rays. It looked like a painting on velvet. "My mother used to say that God had no taste," John commented, looking at it. "I think she might be right."

"Where is she now?"

"Dead."

"Oh. . . ."

He turned away from the window. "As for what we're going to do, it all depends on what you mean. Bixby-wise, we're going to try to use Denver Data as a tool to break into his organization—sneak in the back door, so to speak. I'm certain all of Denver Data has been taken over by him. I'll rummage around there, see if I can use the machine to break the machine."

"What else?"

"Local-wise I think we ought to rummage around here and have a big breakfast ready for Carl and Bev when they get up. Okay? But first I think you ought to get dressed before I go out of my mind. Please."

"That can wait a bit, can't it?" she said coyly. She stood and put her hands in back of her neck and stretched so that her thin robe fell open. His eyes fastened on her breasts. Her whole movement was choreographed to make him feel desire, to make him excited, which it did. He stood, grinning.

"What the hell, breakfast can wait," he said. He took her hand and led her to the bedroom.

Carl Jackson, wartime address New Orleans. Currently living dear Deborgia, Montana. Rural address.

The data operator didn't allow himself to get

carried away. Not yet. Jackson might have moved since last filing his tax return. Still, Montana was close to Wyoming. That looked good. But Jackson was black, and that wasn't so good. Smith might not cross the color lines. Jackson might not cross.

Worth a try, though. He cross-linked into the Montana police computer and put in a request for data on Jackson, working behind the false shield of the Los Angeles police computer and shunting the information before it got into the police network in California.

Carl Jackson, he found, had a speeding ticket eighty-nine days before data request. He was still living in Montana. The operator stabbed the foot switch that alerted the com-net that he needed control and reported to Denver that he had a possible, if not probable, lead.

Denver acknowledged the information. Knowing it went on tape made the operator feel better about his own situation. With control working right there out of Denver—in God's name, why?—it was important to have all information recorded. That way they couldn't drop the load on him if there were any subsequent mistakes.

When the link-up to the memory system in Denver Data was secure he fed through all the information he had on Carl Jackson, including the Montana police report. Then he went back to work on other names from Smith's past.

He had to make certain that as far as his work was concerned there wasn't a possible way for Smith to get away.

John Smith. Christ. That was a name for hotel registers, not for the fuck-up of the entire organization—which was what appeared to be happening.

And it was the guy's real name, too.

EIGHTEEN

After breakfast John explained in detail to Bev and Carl how he was going to try to use the Denver Data system as a tool to infiltrate Bixby's setup. When he was done, sitting at the heavy wood kitchen table, there were several moments of silence. Then Carl coughed lightly for attention.

"Is there a way this man can link you with me?"

"No. Yes—through our army records. But I can't see that happening. They'd have to get our army tie and then take it on down to the present, work out your address—I just don't see them being that thorough. They could, but I don't think they will."

"I was thinking we could send the women away." Carl was looking at the tablecloth.

"I'm staying," Bev said. "Period."

"Where would I go?" Barbara asked. "He's after me, too. If I go hide and something happens here it's just a matter of time anyway. I might as well fight here as in some motel somewhere."

"She has a point," John said. "And I don't think Bev is leaving anyway."

"I'm not." Bev used the back of one hand to

move her long hair back from her face—a very graceful gesture—and John could see the tight set to the sides of her jawline.

"So." Carl said, nodding. "What's next?"

"I go to work." John stood up from the wreckage of scrambled eggs and sausage, but kept his coffee in his hand. "Denver Data opens for regular business at nine—twenty minutes from now. Of course they go twenty-four hours a day. But during normal business hours they're much busier, and there'll be less chance then of them finding out what I'm up to."

He went back to the terminal and sat down. Carl had come with him but the women had stayed behind in the kitchen and John smiled, thinking how ridiculous and homelike it was for Barbara to be helping clear the table and breakfast mess. He thought momentarily of teasing her about it, then decided against it. She'd probably take it wrong and get mad, and he was fast coming to a place in his mind where he no longer wanted to upset her. He was very definitely becoming attached to her. It struck him that he seemed to have known her forever. And yet it had been less then a week.

"So what do we do?" Carl said. He had propped one hip on the storage bins and was studying the numbers on the screen, which meant nothing to him. "What's all that?"

"I'm locked into Denver Data and that's merely the code sequence. Essentially I'm now sitting like I used to sit when I worked there, except that I'm using your terminal and they don't know I'm doing it."

"How can that be? I mean they're sitting there, aren't they? Can't they just plug in and see what you're doing?"

"They could, if they knew where to look and how to look. But I came in from the side, so to speak, and I'm taking out information before they know it's being taken out."

"Sort of like eavesdropping?"

"Exactly like eavesdropping. They could find out if they knew which output to monitor, but there are thousands, hundreds of thousands of places to plug in and they wouldn't know where to start." John snorted. "Besides, I know more about their Goddamn system than they do." He turned to the keyboard again and punched in some new figures.

"What now?" Carl asked.

"Going to see what they know. If they know anything. Then we're going to steal them blind, I hope."

The screen started washing various columns of names and figures—none of which made any sense to Carl—and John watched them slide by. "These are simply various accounts I know about," he said. "I'm just looking for a place to start. Some wild amount of money or something like that to start with. Just smelling around like an old dog, looking for a bone." He kept talking but it was mostly a kind of mental rambling around while he thought.

"Are you looking for anything specific?"

"Sort of. I want to see where the line comes in from Bixby's computer—see if my hunch is right. Bingo."

"What is it?" Carl leaned forward.

"It's a company with a whole bunch of money but it isn't on the preferred list. Usually big companies, where there is privilege involved, are on the preferred list and it takes an extra code to get into them."

"I don't understand why that's unusual—what you've got. I mean none of this makes any sense to me. I'm used to just making orders, you know what I mean?"

"Yeah. But if you know what to look for, all this crap makes sense. It's just numbers and you get used to certain things. Like maybe it doesn't make any difference about this one company, but it *is* out of the ordinary—this company is big bucks and it isn't on the preferred list—so we're going to look at it, see what it's doing."

"I see."

John punched in the identification number for the Shoshone bank as the requesting agency. "That'll throw them off—they'll think the bank out there is making the request for information, if they find out it's being done at all."

A moment passed and the screen was covered with columns of numbers that made no more sense to John than they did to Carl.

"What the hell?" John mused.

"What is it?"

"I don't know. It doesn't mean anything to me. Unless. . . ."

"Unless what?"

"Unless it's a secondary code of some kind that must be broken because we're getting into something important."

He studied the numbers for a time as if waiting for an answer to present itself. Nothing came and he sighed. "No. It's too convoluted for that—it's not a code. It must be something else. Probably just an ID grid system or something."

"I don't know what that is."

"In really big systems, huge computer nets, often a numbered grid is used for identification purposes. We might be into that now. We might be on the line with a big system. Let me renew the demand for information." His voice was tightening without his knowledge as he punched in a new request/demand, still posing as the Shoshone bank.

The screen cleared and came back with a short paragraph of written data.

ALL KNOWN CORRELATIVE CHANNELS WITH SUBJECT BEING EXAMINED. NARROWING TO WESTERN STATES

John closed his eyes. Opened them.

"Your forehead is starting to sweat," Carl said suddenly.

"I'm scared."

"Of that?"

"Right. Of that. I think we're into the main channel of one of Bixby's data links. I think I'm the subject and I'm scared." John rubbed his neck. "They're hunting me now. They're hunting me by finding my friends. They're running me to earth like a Goddamn rabbit...." He trailed off as the image flickered.

The screen wiped clean for a moment and John found himself staring at the statistic printout on Carl Jackson.

"Holy shit." He breathed it.

"What's the matter?" Carl asked.

"Look."

Carl checked the screen. "Goddamn. That's

me!"

"Right."

"But you said they wouldn't make the connection. You said they weren't that smart."

"I was wrong. Damn, Carl, I'm sorry about this. I really didn't know how good his machine was, how much of an organization he had."

"Well, it's done now. Now we've got to get ready."

"To run."

"No. Ain't going to be any running. I've never run from anything in my life and I'm not going to start now."

"Carl...."

"No."

"Carl, they've got your current address. They've got the link between us. They'll come, and this time they'll come hard because of what I did to them the last two times. This guy, Carl, this guy is one mean son of a bitch."

"I'm still not running. They were mean over there, too, and I didn't run but once and that was when we were taking our own fire and then everybody ran."

"They'll come, I tell you. And they'll come big."

"Let me ask you something," Carl stood. "Are you running?"

John thought a moment. "No. But...."

"That's what I mean. And you want me to run?" Carl smiled tightly. "Where would I go? And why? No. I'm staying—shit, this is my place! Did you really think I was going to split?"

"No, I didn't. But I had to try, didn't I? I mean, I had to try."

"I ain't going."

"I know. Now we get to fight."

"I'll start making this place into a Goddamn firebase." Carl stood of the box he'd been leaning against. "You stay with it on the computer end and see what you can do, right? I've got two thoughts first, though."

"What?" John turned.

"First, can we get the women out?"

"We could try, but they wouldn't go. At least Barbara wouldn't go. I don't know about Bev, of course. I don't think. . . ." John paused.

"Don't think what?"

"If we die, they die."

"That's cold, man."

"I know, but that's the way it is, right? This bastard will stay with it. Either we stop Bixby here, or he goes all the way. If the women run and we stay and Bixby wipes us, he'll go after them anyway, right? Where can they go that he won't find them sooner or later? And he's got to take them out—he's got to take us all out. So they might as well stay. We've got to win here, at this place."

"But do we have to win alone?"

"What do you mean?"

"How about the cops?" Carl made a motion with his hands. "That's the other thing. Is there some reason we can't call them?"

"No. We can call them. It just won't do any good—Bixby is into the police computer, can insert data. If we call the cops and tell them our names, they'll probably get the law's word that we're crazy, police buffs who give false reports all the time. That's what happened last time."

"Ahhh." Carl nodded. "I see. So. We're going to do it alone this time."

"Yes. Unless I can bust into his system and then work back into the police system on my own, erase it, and change it all. Then we can call the cops. But. . . ."

"That will take a long time."

"Yes."

"It will take too long."

"Probably. He'll be here soon—we don't know how long he's had that data about you. They could be here any minute."

"I'd better get it going, then." But he hung for a moment in the door and John looked at him.

"What's the matter?" John asked.

"You know all that time outside Danang at Firebase Alpha when they were coming at us a lot?"

John winced. Hot-white zips of death, screams, little pops, meat-hit sounds; ducking and never talking and waiting and sweating while you waited. "Yeah. I remember it. I try not to, but I do. Why?"

"I was scared then."

"So was I. So was everybody."

"No. I mean I was really scared. When they came out of the tree-line that time and there were so many of them I about lost it."

"I *did* lose it. All I could do was pray over and over. I'm not even sure I fired."

Carl studied him. "Really? You aren't just saying that?"

"No. I remember when it was over I felt my barrel and it was cool and it should have been hot. I think I thought I was shooting, but I wasn't. So what are you worried about?"

"Nothing." Carl smiled. "Ain't we a pair? Waiting for this Bixby?"

"Shit, man," John said. "It's the fear that makes you mean, right? Brave people die."

"Brave people die. Right."

"So let's get scared and whip the crap out of Bixby."

"Yeah. I'll start digging. You see if you can find out from that box when they're coming."

John nodded and turned to work and Carl went outside to start digging. You didn't fight from houses unless you were in the movies. You fought from the earth. Only the earth could protect you and stop the popping death—only the earth could save you.

Or bury you.

NINETEEN

You needed only one phone line to blow people away, John thought, looking at the screen. If people knew how insecure their money was in a computer banking system, they would live in constant terror. All a knowledgeable thief needed was one line into a data system and he could steal it blind.

All John needed for his own purposes was one line.

And he had it.

Now, if he could make a valid request it would open a door for him into Bixby's crime computer—wherever it was—and then he could dig in and raise some hell. No, more than some—a lot of hell.

Right now, with the line he had, he could eavesdrop. But he didn't know the code sequence which would allow him to make demands on the system. He couldn't make the "valid request." He needed that code.

He gambled. At the top of the data printout that had flashed information about Carl was a standard ID—a series of numbers and letters that represented the requesting agency. Since Carl's terminal lacked a memory system in which to store the ID, John jotted it down on a pad.

The ID, originating in Denver, probably had no priority, he thought, but it was a start.

He keyed the ID into the terminal. He was now locked into the data line between the requesting computer in Denver and the one issuing the information on Carl—wherever it was located. Neither of the two systems knew he was there and, until he got caught, he could issue information or request it without revealing his identity; each of them would think the data was coming from the other. He would get caught, he knew, as soon as one of them smelled a rat because he was seeing information he didn't request, or as soon as one of them, for any reason, demanded that he establish his identity in code. But why look for trouble before it happened?

He used the ID and asked for more information concerning Carl Jackson.

STANDBY ONE

The answer came so fast, so immediate, that John knew somebody was monitoring the data line all the time. Not just a computer, but a man. That meant the requesting ID *did* have priority.

There was a little nudge in the corner of his brain. He was onto something. Maybe.

FURTHER INFORMATION CARL JACKSON BEING COMPILED AS PER CONTROL REQUEST. REGRET CANNOT COMPLY UNTIL COMPILATION COMPLETE

What kind of hokey shit is this, John thought.

Regret? Why would an issuing computer go through all that fancy language just to tell somebody to wait a minute? It was silly.

Control?

What was that? No—*who* was that? The nudge grew, spread, became a hunch. Control was somebody big, somebody with a lot of clout. Somebody in Denver.

"Holy Jesus jumping. . . ."

Barbara came walking into the room at that moment with a cup of coffee in her hand. "I thought you might need this before I go out to help Carl and Bev dig—what's the matter?"

"I'm Bixby."

"What?"

"No shit. I'm locked into Bixby's computer. I just got lucky and saw his identification number and used it and the computer thinks I'm Bixby. I can order it to do anything I want."

"For how long?"

"Minutes. Maybe less. Until he finds out and changes the code. No, wait. Christ, *I* can change the code!" He concentrated on the keyboard, forgetting she was there, and typed in new program orders, using Bixby's own ID as the ordering justification.

By changing the ID to a sequence of numbers of his own choosing, he effectively "stole" the computer from Bixby. As soon as he did this, he erased the ordering information before it could appear on remote screens. He thought for a moment.

Time was limited. In a short while his code change would be discovered; the opposition would make a concentrated effort to break the new code and he would be out of the picture.

How could he best use the stolen moments?

"I have to go back out and help them dig," Barbara cut in. She'd been standing in the doorway all this time. He nodded at her but didn't look up again, only sensed that she'd gone.

First find the monster, the controlling crime computer. He requested its location.

LAX, came the answer.

John's eyes gleamed. The computer was using one of the abbreviations for Los Angeles, the same one that the airlines used. So it was in L.A. But Bixby was in Denver, at the other data center. Of course! He didn't have to be near his monster, didn't want to be; it could go right on automatically ingesting data and relaying commands while he lived a private, shielded life hundreds of miles away!

John requested a breakdown by location of all the data centers used in Bixby's network and watched as the screen laid a pattern of lines and boxes. Each box was a data center feeding the main one in Los Angeles. The location of each center was printed in the middle of its box—like a block schematic diagram.

Los Angeles. Denver. Dallas. Boston. Miami. Minneapolis. Toronto. Geneva. Frankfurt.

"God. He's all over." John punched in a request for subfeeds, one station at a time, to show for just two seconds each. Rapidly, but so that he could still read them, the screen began to flash diagrams of all the sub-data centers—banks, businesses, government agencies, more!—that were feeding the main crime computer. The network was worldwide, immense. Little links here, big ones there—there was nothing Bixby had missed.

His original computer system had stolen the others, taken them over one by one without their owners' knowledge. The network had grown so huge as to have hooks into every powerful financial institution in the world!

"The whole world." John breathed. "It's everywhere." Like a disease!

He watched, fascinated. Even as he watched, the links were being updated. The screen was flashing new lines tied into new banks that meant new accounts were being rifled. New crimes of all sorts were taking place, automatically ordered, then automatically erased by the main crime computer in L.A. as soon as they'd been committed, so that they appeared never to have occurred. It was awesome.

"The man is committing crimes he doesn't even know about," John said to himself, staring at the screen, watching the diagrams rippling past. "He's taking it all. The computer is just taking it all. Billions."

The concept became even more stunning as John thought more about it. Bixby had programmed his original computer to commit a series of standard computer crimes that never reached the point where they'd be noticed. But then, as an added touch—what had happened? had he gotten bored?—he'd keyed the computer into a growth pattern that had enabled it to become an integrated part of its own program!

Then Bixby had just leaned back to rake it in. Probably the link back to Geneva went into a numbered account. Conceivably, he was reinvesting the enormous sums he was reaping. Enormous—shit, John thought, enormous was hardly the word for it! The harvest was uncountable, growing at such a geometric rate and at such speeds that Bixby probably had no idea how much he was worth.

He could be stealing from himself, John thought with a tight smile. Hell, he might even own a couple of the banks he was rifling.

And it was all threatened by him—by John Smith, sitting at a mail-order ranch in Montana. Something had rippled; a diode had blown and sent out an order that had caused screw-ups everywhere. God knows how much damage had been done to Bixby's setup, but John was certain that what he'd discovered at the Shoshone bank was only one of the fallouts.

He himself had become one part of an error that had to be rectified.

Well, Goddamn, he was one part that wasn't going to be that easy to rectify! He was going to make such an unholy mess of the whole system that Bixby—even if he killed him—would *never* get it working right again.

But first, he owed Carl Jackson something for what he'd done for him, owed him a lot, and he intended to pay a debt of gratitude right now. Smiling as he tapped at the keyboard, John requested all western area banks holding Bixby's accounts to be put on display. The screen showed Bixby had major accounts in seven western states—the biggest in Utah. John didn't take time to check on the amounts in each. He simply ordered all the funds in all the banks shunted into Carl's account at the First National bank in Missoula, Montana, the number of which was taped to the console. He waited a moment for verification, tapping his thumbs impatiently on the side of the console.

Time was running out. Bixby would soon know of the change of codes and the shit was sure to hit the fan.

Verification came. John hadn't asked for the total sum involved, knew only that it was considerable. He left it to Carl to work out an explanation for his bank, if he needed one, of the major influx of funds—he could tell them of a merger or something. That's if somebody at the bank raised the question, which, banks being what they were, was unlikely.

With that job done, John thought another moment, then nodded grimly to himself. The best way to kill a snake was to cut the head off. He'd already scotched the snake by taking charge of the computer temporarily. That wasn't enough. He needed to take a crack at removing the whole Goddamn thing from Bixby's control permanently.

Taking a deep breath, John ordered the whole system to make a complete data dump—effectively ordering each and every computer and substation to commit suicide by erasing itself.

CANNOT COMPLY.

The screen glowed the letters.

"Yeah, well, it was worth a shot," John muttered aloud.

He realized then what perhaps he might have guessed all along, that Bixby would have, of course, built in protective measures against a data dump order. But if he hadn't, he could have wiped him out with one move—so the gamble was well worth the time spent on it.

He thought some more. So he couldn't cut the head off. Bixby was smart, had anticipated somebody attacking him frontally. But he was vulnerable to sneak attacks from the side. For instance, he had to allow transfers—the whole system worked on the principle of transferring money and material. There was no way Bixby could stop transfers from taking place without shutting down the entire system.

STANDBY

The screen flashed abruptly, erasing the previous CANNOT COMPLY statement. It was on to his threat to it, was trying to regain control of itself, fighting him all the way. Whether it was the computer or the man at the console doing it John didn't know. But it hardly mattered.

Battle was joined, either way. He had to jump now, jump ahead of them.

John changed the code, punched in all new numbers, trying in that manner to stay a few minutes ahead of Bixby's catching up with him. He thought another moment.

He could steal anything and everything, but he needed a place to "put" it all. He needed a memory system someplace to send all the data to, for storage. When he had it all he could erase it. Actually, he could erase it as it was *being* transferred, as it came in.

He smiled. The Denver Data Center, his old place, had a computer with a memory bank he could use. He could put stuff into that system, run through the storage process, then erase it—which was to say, feed all the data back into a system controlled by Bixby and then wipe it out.

Kill the snake by feeding it to itself.

"Perfect," he breathed. He was working fast now, typing requests and program changes with great speed. The sweat on his forehead was not from the heat of the steadily rising sun—it promised to be a baking hot day—but from the pressure of staying ahead of Bixby; he had no way of knowing if Bixby knew he was inside the system tearing it apart, knew only that he had to hurry.

To elude Bixby's possible probes, to stay just that one jump ahead of him, he came up with a stroke of genius. He worked up a mini-program through the Denver Center that would automatically change the identification he was using at one-minute intervals and would change the requesting orders at the same rate. That way, until Bixby himself caught on, hopefully, he would be working just ahead of the searching computer. That was for self-protection—he still had to fight, to do damage. But while fighting, he would be escaping—maybe, because it was kind of like trying to run sideways in Crisco fat.

He started to transfer money, companies and all other Bixby-stolen data to Denver Data for immediate censure after acceptance. The system computers sending the data on his request responded without question, reading it as a normal transaction. The Denver receiving system also meekly complied with the orders. It was working. Given a little time, maybe as little as half an hour, and John could wipe out Bixby's entire fortune. He could build it up again, but all that he had worked for would be erased, all of it, and he would need much time. Time in which the authorities could be brought in to stop him permanently.

"One more thing," John reminded himself. He had to knock off the link to the Goddamn criminal data system in Washington/Maryland and erase that bullshit about him being a police buff or a crazy, whatever it was Bixby had put in. He had to find that link and erase it. So then and there he ordered a scan of the programs out of the Los Angeles computer so as to find the link.

The screen when dead.

"Damn. Fuse must have blown. . ." At first, he really thought that was what had happened, so engrossed had he become in his work. The fuse or breaker in Carl's terminal must have blown, cutting off all power. Then he saw that the power light on the console was still glowing and that the in-house system was still functioning.

It was the telephone line that was dead.

He checked and rechecked all his connections. They were okay. But nothing—no signal going out or coming in.

"It's as if the line's been cut," he said, and then realized that that was exactly what had happened. "Damn."

They were here. Already. They were down at the driveway entrance off the highway and they'd cut the telephone lines prior to coming up at them.

He stood up just as Carl came bursting through the front door. "I heard engines," Carl said. "Maybe one chopper."

"They're here already," John said, nodding.

"How could they make it so fast?"

"It doesn't matter."

"No. It doesn't." John followed him to the door, trotting. "You all set?"

"Got two L-shaped trenches and an escape run that might work."

"Might?"

"Yeah. Might. We didn't have time for much more—you complaining?"

"Sure. Bitch, bitch, bitch—you know me." They were outside on the porch, running.

"Weapons?" John asked.

"Everything I could find is in the trenches."

"Did you remember my Sharps?"

"Yeah—and that box of ammo."

"Field of fire?"

"The best," Carl said, stopping for a moment and listening. The engines were louder now—there was apparently a truck—and the definite whuf-*whuf* of a helicopter could be heard. "They'll be here in three or four minutes."

"Shit," John said, half smiling. "It's just like old times, isn't it?"

"Yeah," Carl answered. "And shit is the right word."

"We're going to stop them," John said, running, and damn near piled into Carl when the latter stopped and turned again.

"No," Carl said. His face was serious. There was was fear showing in his eyes, but it was the controlled kind of fear that could be used, something very far from panic. "We won't stop them. If they come very hot we won't be able to, not just two of us on guns. But we're going to hurt them, John. We're going to get killed. But before that we're going to hurt them *bad*, and that's straight."

Then he turned and ran up into the pines, up into the middle of the green, soft, warm Montana mountains that were so lovely and which made no sense at all to John in their present situation. No more than would the music of Sibelius if played in a slaughterhouse.

"Holy mother of God," the daytime data operator said. He was still holding the phone that he had been hung up on, terrified, trying desperately to recall the sequence of events that had led up to this moment.

He'd come on duty at eight A.M. in relief of the night operator, who said he'd been shit at all through his shift, and looked it.

As was routine with him, he had sipped his coffee and thumbed through a girlie magazine at the console. He remembered distinctly doing that for perhaps fifteen or twenty minutes. No, more than twenty. Maybe a lot less. Probably quite a bit less. He wanted to be really sure about that because now he had to prove to control that it was not he who was on duty when it started happening.

Immediately after his coffee and magazine perusal, he'd done a regular program check and had gotten a no-entry.

He couldn't get into more than two-thirds of the sections on his own computer. Or on control's own computer. The others wouldn't answer him. What's more, there was a massive transfer of data going on, a steady pumping of it out to Denver. But when he'd called Denver on the com-net they didn't know anything about it.

Just acknowledged that it was coming in, had no idea why.

It was all very strange. Then it became very frightening. Because when he'd finally gotten a patch through to control, he'd been blasted first by a stream of obscenities and then by a cold announcement that, barring an exonerating explanation by him, he was a dead man.

By then practically all of it had been gutted. Maybe all of it—the whole system. Only one thing was sure: when the smoke settled control would be coming to get his ass for it. He was going to have to prove it had happened on the night shift, and not while he was looking at a magazine picture of pretty Tanya with the silicone breasts.

TWENTY

The spot Carl had selected was a large patch of tree-dotted grass, like a park, just below the top of the ridge in back of the house. From it you could see the whole valley sloping down to the main highway. Much of this valley was covered with Ponderosa pines, obscuring the view of the road, but some of it was open meadowland, to which elk came down from the mountain to feed in the fall and winter. Looking across these meadows you could see for miles.

Carl and the women had dug two shallow L-shaped trenches, with the long ends almost touching and in the shape of a crude zig-zag. The trenches were only deep enough to crouch in, whereas a good firebase would be deep enough for standing. But they made for good cover and concealment, far enough up and away from the house to give them time to prepare.

There were guns everywhere. In the sort time he'd had, Carl had stripped the house of weapons and ammo. There were three shotguns, two pumps and one double-barrel, three .30-'06 rifles, and four muzzle-loading rifles. Also John saw three handguns lying in front of the trench. Down in the corner of the far L there were boxes of ammunition for all of the weapons. In the rough middle between the L's,

Barbara and Bev sweated over shovels.

Barbara was smiling. "I haven't worked like this. . .in a long time. Since before."

"You did good," John said, answering the smile. "It's a good firebase."

"Engine's getting louder," Carl said. "They'll be here soon."

John nodded, jumped down in the trench and checked weapons for loading. They were all hot, including his Sharps, which was leaning in the corner with the other rifles. Cartridges in all of them, chamber and magazines. Even the muzzle-loaders were loaded and capped. John nodded. They had worked hard.

"How do you see it?" he asked Carl.

Carl thought. "I make it as a hold and withdraw number. We try to take a few each time we stop to hold. We can't pull a Custer and stay here and get wiped."

"But we're in good shape," Bev cut in. "You said we were with this trench."

"We are," John answered. He noted that Barbara was studying him quietly, as she'd studied him on the mountainside when he'd killed the man. A speculative look. He said, "This way we can fight a little—the other way we would have died instantly. But we still can't beat an organized force. . . ."

He quit talking as the helicopter got increasingly louder and then came into view over in the meadow, about three-quarters of a mile below them. It was the two-man kind of chopper, with the big bug-eyed bubble out in front, and it hovered back and forth slowly—like something prehistoric looking for prey.

"They're going back and forth as they approach the house," John said, his voice tightening. "They want to make sure we don't get away. Bastards." He turned to Carl. "I don't make the truck yet—do you?"

"No. Big, though. Maybe a one-ton. It's still back on the drive somewhere and hasn't broken out of the trees yet...."

"We've got to act now," John said. "We can't let them have the initiative."

"I know." Carl turned to Bev. "You know that place where the three big Ponderosas hang over the stream, where we made love that time?"

She nodded.

"You take her." He pointed to Barbara. "You go now. We're going to bust a few and then we'll come there. Take shotguns, one each, and a box of ammo each."

"I can't shoot," Barbara said.

"It's for them," Bev said. "When they get there."

She jumped out of the trench and took the shotguns and shells and started off at an easy trot. "Come on," she said to Barbara, but Barbara hung back.

"Am I going to see you again?" She asked John and tried to keep her voice steady.

"You're kidding," John said. He smiled. "That's right out of the movies."

"Well, I just wanted to know. You know. I felt...you know. I just felt."

"I know. I felt it too. I'll get there, don't worry."

She left, half-believing, and Carl issued a quiet laugh. "Liar."

"So what the hell," John said, looking out

across the valley. "We might make it."

"Right. Because our hearts are pure and our strength is the strength of ten. . . ."

But John wasn't listening. He was instead studying the far edge of the valley—almost a basin, really, surrounded by trees—and after a moment he put a hand on Carl's arm. "What do you make it across to the trees?"

"In yards or meters?"

"Get serious."

"Six hundred to seven hundred yards. Maybe a bit more."

"That's what I make it. Doesn't the driveway run along that edge on the way up to the house?"

"Yeah. Out around the basin—where you going?"

"Down below," John called back. He'd grabbed the Sharps and the box of shells and jumped out of the trench. "I'm going to lay a little long-range fire on them and try to slow them down. This bastard throws so much smoke I'll do it down below so as not to give away our position."

He disappeared down the slope, around a stand of boulders, as Carl nodded.

John ran downhill at a trot, watching the far edge all the while. It was two hundred yards to the bottom of the slope, to the edge of the basin, and that reduced the range of firing to perhaps five hundred yards. Still one hell of a distance, he thought, but he should be able to do some damage.

At the bottom of the slope, on the edge of the basin but still slightly higher than the other side, there was a deadfall pine knocked over by an ancient wind, but not killed. It was still growing, but so far over as to be almost sideways—like a horizontal, huge green bush.

"Perfect," John said, and burrowed into the branches on the near side, picking a place where a hole went through so he could see. There was a limb of some size there—he was close to the trunk end—and he situated himself so the limb would be right for resting the heavy barrel of the Sharps on.

The engines were very loud now. There were two rigs coming, he guessed. He worked fast. He set the sight for a full six hundred yards—he always underjudged range—and slid a round in and raised the block, never taking his eyes off the far side of the meadow.

The chopper had gone on ahead, doing recon up by the house. There was a sudden burst of firing, a quick rattle over the whuff-*whuf* of the blades and he guessed they'd run into the dogs. Carl had made the dogs stay when the four of them had run so they wouldn't give away positions and John felt a sudden pang for Carl. He'd loved the dogs like children and there was no reason to kill them—they knew nothing of computers. They were just animals.

His mind was drifting, the way it always had before fighting. Back then.

Over the quick chatter of automatic weapons he now heard the stomach-thumping roar of a heavier rifle and knew that Carl had decided to try to take the helicopter out with one of the ought-sixes. He smiled. He knew Carl wasn't going to simply wait while he worked the meadow. Carl had never waited like that in his life.

Four times the big rifle thumped but the whuf-*whuf* continued, back around out of sight at the house, so he must have missed the pilot and rotor. Still, somebody was going to get hurt, John knew—Carl was big, and awfully good at shooting. His huge frame made him a nearly perfect gun platform and shots that didn't hit were always very close. John would not want to be inside the helicopter.

A truck appeared across the meadow.

It was a rental truck, a two-ton stakebed, and in the back John could just make out three men with what appeared to be motorcycles. Dirt bikes. He allowed a quick flick of admiration for Bixby's organization to go through his mind; Bixby had come ready for anything. Then he settled his hooded front sight on the side window of the truck's leading edge and squeezed the set trigger.

He couldn't see where the shot struck because of the smoke and the range, but the truck slewed over into the side of the driveway and stopped, so he assumed he'd taken the driver.

There was no time now for thinking. Had to fire and withdraw. Take out what was possible while he could, then haul ass.

Without thinking he loaded, selected one of the men in back who was standing and fighting the drop gate. Another squeeze and the hammer came down. The pure lead slug slammed out and across the meadow and took the man in the chest and wiped him off the truck the way bugs are wiped off tables. The man was dead and gone.

John loaded and fired four more times,

chunking the big slugs into the truck and any target that showed. Then he heard the little pops that meant they were returning fire, shooting at the huge cloud of black powder smoke in front of him and his tree. He nodded, dropped down and ran quickly back up the slope to the trenches.

Carl was just getting back to the trench after his attempt to take out the helicopter and John threw him a quick greeting. "Did you get it?"

Carl shook his head. "I think I took out the passenger but I missed the pilot. Goddamn bubble must have deflected the bullets a little. Or something."

"I took some of them out," John said. "Across the meadow. But there are more. I made eight, maybe nine of them, and they've got dirt bikes."

"I hear."

There was the sudden, guttural cough and wail of two-cycle engines being started. The two men watched the basin and saw first one, then two more dirt bikes come out across the grass.

"Use the ought-sixes," Carl said, raising his rifle. "The scopes are set for three hundred, for hunting mountain elk."

John nodded, grabbed a rifle from the corner and propped it on the side of the trench. It took him two seconds to find anything in the four-power scope. Then he found the man and the bike but saw both snatched away before he could squeeze, slammed down when Carl's rifle thundered next to him.

"Bastards. Shoot my dogs, bastards." Carl was murmuring as he fired, working the bolt and squeezing them off with precision, selecting new targets as if he was working at a range.

John didn't get a round off. Before he could get settled on a target and fire, Carl had cleaned the meadow out. The last bike flipped in the air when the driver was hit and the engine whined a few seconds before dropping back to an idle. No bike made it closer than two hundred yards to the bottom of the slope in front of them, not anywhere near the tree line, and John didn't fire a shot.

"Jesus, Carl, that was some shooting."

"Bastards shouldn't have taken my dogs like that. No reason." Carl was reloading, his face wet and black in the heat from the sun and from his hot rifle, the huge hands delicately slipping the new rounds down into the clip.

Out in the meadow one of the men by a dirt bike moved, tried to get up, then either fell or dropped back for cover behind the bike. Carl raised his rifle, rested it, let out half a breath and squeezed. The elk load—one hundred and eighty grains of semi-jacketed slug—took out part of the bike and most of the man's skull.

"Easy, Carl. Easy." John said, keeping his voice low.

"Fuck that shit. You brought them here and you want me to take it easy? Blow it out your ass."

John nodded. Carl was close to losing control of himself, and you couldn't do that and live. "For you, man, not for me. Remember Boggs?"

Carl stared at him, then slowly smiled and nodded. "Old Boggs, he couldn't hold anything but his water, could he?"

Boggs had been a corporal from the swamps

down in Louisiana. He got pissed off every single time they got into a fire-fight or took anything incoming. He would stand and swear at them, didn't seem to feel fear, and he was standing and swearing for the last time when he took an incoming eighty-deuce mortar round about two feet from his right side. They didn't find anything in that area but Bogg's helmet and a red mist.

"Yeah. I'm okay now," Carl said. "I'm all right."

John nodded again, studied the meadow.

The truck was still in the ditch alongside the road on the far side. They were taking fire from one or two men in back of it, but the fire was directed well below them. The shooters still couldn't be seen readily; they were shooting around the smoke cloud John had put out with the Sharps.

A second vehicle suddenly appeared, a four-wheel-drive pickup—also a rental—and there were two men in the cab and two in the back with a stock rack and horses. Two, maybe three horses.

"Son of a bitch has an army," Carl said. "I can't believe this."

"I should have told you," John said. "When I was at your terminal trying to wipe his programs, I took a look at the size of his network. He's everywhere—he just might have an army. . . ."

The helicopter's rotor blades suddenly grew louder. The chopper had been moving in the other direction as it searched for where Carl was thought to have run, but the people in the truck had a radio and had called it back.

The sound receded, then got still louder as the chopper shot off to their side out into the meadow. Unbelievably, miraculously, the pilot hadn't seen them in the trench. The chopper moved over to the truck, settled in by it but kept its engine going at a rate close to lift. The truck and chopper men were having a confab, John saw, too close to them for comfort.

"It's just a matter of time," he said, watching.

"Yeah. We'd better cut out of here," Carl said. "I forgot to tell you—the trees where the women will be are off a mile at about two-ninety degrees, almost dead northwest. In case we get separated."

"Never happen."

"Never happen."

"Let's lay a little fire on them and get out...." John raised the ought-six he was holding, settled the scope on the helicopter motor assembly and fired five rounds as rapidly as he could. He reloaded and put in five more but he couldn't see any damage—though the helicopter didn't rise. Carl's rifle thundered simultaneously, at the same target. They were both hitting but at that range nothing showed; the chopper rotors kept turning.

All other targets were hidden or down—both trucks were empty and the men stayed in the ditch on the far side.

Carl stopped firing. John fired two more rounds into the chopper and then did the same. He studied the area across the meadow through his scope.

"I can't see any of them."

"We've quit taking fire," Carl said. "I don't get it. I *know* we didn't kill all of them...."

Two rounds suddenly hit well above their position, maybe forty feet up from them. They weren't directed and amounted to little more than harassment. Neither of the men could see where the rounds had come from.

"Looks like they're trying to keep us here and down," Carl said.

"So they can work around to the side?" John wondered.

Carl snorted. "Hell, it'd take them a week." He was watching through the scope and he squeezed off a round. "Might have been something just to the right of the truck in the ditch—maybe a head. Worth a shot."

"Always." John nodded. Shoot everything all the time. Don't think, just shoot. Shoot all things and maybe you'll live. Just maybe. Bushes, dirt, open places, all things. Keep up fire.

"They're waiting for something." John pumped another general purpose round into the helicopter—the pilot had long since jumped out the far side and made for the ditch.

"Yeah—but that ain't part of the program. They should be assaulting. They could have had us if they'd kept coming. What are they waiting for?"

"Don't know, don't know...." John swung his scope sideways up both sides of the meadow, all around through the trees, looking deep, trying to see. "I can't make anything. Nothing."

"What time is it?" Carl asked.

"Coming up on noon," John said, glancing at his watch.

"Getting hot. You figure they're going to sweat us out?"

John shook his head. "No need. It's something else."

"That Bixby asshole, he's going to be mad if they don't take us pretty soon." Carl laughed.

"Yeah. John dropped back into the trench and took a canteen—Carl had four of them, the big kind covered with wet wool to keep them cool—and held some water in his mouth before swallowing. He frowned in thought, the creases in his brow drawing light lines in the sweat and dust there. "How long you figure we've been up here?" he asked.

"Ten minutes," Carl said, smiling, "or an hour, or a week. Fact is, I lost my watch."

"It's not over an hour and a half since we moved up here. But they've got a radio down there and probably phones in some of those rigs and in the chopper too. That man I busted down in Wyoming had a phone."

"So?"

"So they're in touch with Bixby all the time. So he's giving them orders."

"And he told them to quit attacking?"

John nodded. "That's how I figure it."

"Why? The son of a bitch has us dead. Why hold back?"

"Because he needs us alive. He needs *me* alive."

"Oh yeah? For what? Something to play with?"

"No. I changed all his codes. I tore apart his

TWENTY-ONE

The women weren't there.

Carl came abreast of John after they'd run a few hundred yards. He led him at a dogtrot down to the dry bottom of a short, small canyon and then up a shallow slope to where three huge ponderosas stood near the crown of a rock-covered hill. Back when the country had been logged off, these three trees had been left; virgin timber several hundred years old, they stood like kings over the rest of the forest.

But the women were nowhere to be seen.

Carl called and John started to do the same but his throat closed. He put a hand on Carl's arm. "Quit it. They aren't here."

"Sure they are. She knew right where to come and I sent her and she's here but she just doesn't hear me...."

"They're not here."

Carl turned, grabbed John by the shoulders, picked him off the ground and held him, canteens, rifles and all, a foot in the air. "She's *here*, Goddamn it!"

John said nothing but simply hung until the mad fire went down in Carl's eyes. Carl put him back down on the ground gently but with great, vital force.

"It's my fault," John said. "Bixby has been ahead of me on every Goddamn turn, every single one."

"They must have seen the women leave the trench." Carl squatted on the ground. "That's why the helicopter was out of sight for such a long time while we were taking out those bikers. They went after the women. Shit."

"No. It's my fault." John was still winded from the long trot. He fell against a small tree and let himself slide to the ground. "They're reading my mail. They've got me all around. I can't think ahead of them."

Carl said nothing. He looked out down the small valley they'd just run through. "We'll have to go back."

"No." John shook his head. "*I'll* have to go. It was my Goddamn fault and it's me Bixby wants—I'll go back. Maybe we can negotiate—they'll swap the women for me."

"Right." Carl spit in the dust. Wiped the sweat from his forehead. "You and the Goddamn tooth fairy. They gotta kill us all, you know that. We go back and they take us all out. And we gotta go back...."

John shook his head but said nothing. There was nothing to say. It looked as if they were caught between the rock and the hard place. The hot sun cooked him out and he felt weak and smelled himself and none of it, none of it was working.

"We've got to do something," Carl said.

"I know."

"We can't just sit here."

"I know."

"Well, Goddamn it, *do* it!"

John looked up at him. His face was soaked and shining. "I'm thinking. I was thinking." He stood slowly, his legs taking the load of his body gradually. "I'm tired."

"Yeah. I know what you mean," Carl said. "But that doesn't change anything."

"I wasn't bitching—just stating a fact."

"Sorry." But Carl's voice was bitter and John knew he wasn't sorry but was instead worrying deeply about what was going to happen to the women.

"Way I figure it," John said, "is we have to run to his hand. Or at least we have to appear to be running to his hand."

"Explain."

"The way things have been going, he's got to think I'm stupid, right? I mean he's been one jump ahead of me all the way. So we've got to go with that."

"So he's right, you're stupid," Carl said. "So what? How can that help us?"

"We've got to go back," John said, starting back down the way they'd come. "Let's walk while I talk—I don't think we've got much time."

Carl followed, moved off to the side a few feet and matched John's slower pace. "What's the plan?"

John plodded along. "It's pretty Goddamn basic. We've got to kill Bixby."

"No shit, iron horse."

"Yeah. I know how that sounds. But I think if we can somehow take the bastard out the rest of it will crumble like rotten cake. I think. Those people all work for him for money and if they see him gone they aren't going to be too loyal, right?"

"But dammit, John, we know all that—that doesn't help. We can't get close to him. You said he was smarter than us. You think he's going to let you get close to him?"

"No. *You're* going to kill him."

"That's nice to know. How?"

"I'm going to set him up and you're going to punch his ticket. I go in like I'm young and dumb and tell them that you were hit when we ran. That way, I set him up for you. If it all works just right we might get one shot. *You* might get one shot."

"Might."

"Yes. Might." John stopped and readjusted the sling on the ought-six he was carrying. "Carl, I'll say it again—I've never been so sorry for something I've done. If there was a way to make it all not have happened. . .ahh, hell, you know all this."

"Yeah." Carl's voice softened. "I know you didn't figure on all this when you came up. And you know I don't mind—we're watash, right? Shit, man, you don't stick with your friends you don't stick with nothing. I'm just worried about Bev, is all, and Barbara." He looked at the sky, a flat blue bowl with light blue heat that worked down on them. "I lose that thing with Bev and I might be all my life trying to find something like it again."

"Then don't miss," John said, looking at his friend closely. "If I get him out where you can hit him, for God's sake don't miss."

"*John Smith: We have the women!*"

John nodded. They had a public address system, either on the helicopter or in one of the trucks with the CB radios. The sound boomed across the meadow, tore at the soft mountain grass and the pine needles like thunder.

"John Smith and Carl Jackson: We have the women! Come out now and they won't be harmed!"

Carl and John had come back to the meadow from the side, working carefully through the trees, maintaining close cover until they were back to the tree where John had started action with the Sharps. The bikes and bodies were still strewn in the grass and John could see clouds of flies over them. Always that, always with death there were flies; sickening blue, shiny, filthy fucking flies.

"You got a good field of fire?" John whispered, without looking down to where Carl hid in the tight branches of the tree. "You ready?"

"Yeah. I got all I can get. It'll have to do." Carl was almost under the tree, the rifle wedged tightly, solidly, his eye glued to the scope. "I don't make Bixby though. Or anybody else. No new people or machinery."

"Come out John Smith and Carl Jackson!"

"So we wait," John whispered. "It's no good without Bixby."

John had rubbed dirt on his face to cut the shine, and the sweat had made rivulets down through the dirt. It would have looked comical in some other situation—this whole thing would have been comical in some other situation, he thought, staring across the meadow at the trucks and helicopter. They must have hit the rotor assembly or the pitch control rods, because the engine had been stopped. Trucks, helicopters, assault bikes—Bixby had a private social structure going, a little world within the real world with an army and an economy, all of it. A little king.

Only not so little.

"I hate waiting," John heard Carl say after four or five minutes.

"Yeah." But it changed nothing to hate it. Like hunting elk on a stationary stand hunt. You could hate standing and waiting for the elk to come out into range—sometimes it took days to get a shot—but you still had to do it. If you wanted the elk.

"The women are down in the ditch," John said. "I caught a flash of Bev's hair." He stood higher than the spot where Carl lay and had a slightly better angle. "Couldn't see Barbara...." She was there, though. Bixby would want her alive and well, so he could do her himself. Son of a bitch.

Anger tightened his neck and shoulder muscles and he fought it away. He couldn't be angry, had to put the mad down or he'd react instead of act, and he had to do everything right this time.

"Chopper," Carl said. He always had been able to hear better. In Nam he could hear the evac choppers when they were still only thinking about coming. "Coming fast."

"Bixby," John said, nodding. "So far so good." He thought a moment. All right. I'll try to set Bixby up but as soon as you shoot I'm going to get a weapon and add to the fire. You keep it up and I'll try to fight the women out."

"A whole lot of trying talk going on there," Carl said.

"It's all we've got," John answered. "It's like a toothache—we've got to make it so bad they won't have any choice but to go to the dentist. If we make it all shit for them and they see Bixby is dead, they'll split."

"You hope."

"You got that right." Jargon. Singsong of military Nam talk. It helped. But John knew it would take more than cocky talk to beat this mother. This one counted. He was just now realizing how much it counted when he thought of Barbara and what Bixby would do to her.

"Here he comes," Carl said.

Another bubble chopper came up over the small ridge that ran along the back side of the driveway. It hovered slowly, as if studying the crippled helicopter, then made a circle and landed up the drive—towards the house a bit—from the trucks. Two men got out and ran to the ditch in back of the trucks—too fast for John to identify them, not that it would have done any good. He had no idea what Bixby looked like. He had to bet on it and get lucky.

"What's written on the side of the chopper?" John said.

"Mountain Helicopter Rental." Carl was reading through the scope. "It's in Missoula—about eighty miles."

"Bastard rents everything," John mused, waiting.

"*John Smith and Carl Jackson come on out. We have the women.*"

"Well," John said. "I'd better get my ass in gear."

"As the duchess said to the archbishop," Carl said, but he wasn't smiling. "Good luck, you know what I mean?"

"I can dig it," John answered, nodding. "See you."

He stepped out and away from the tree and started across the meadow. He walked slowly, dropping his rifle immediately and holding his hands well out to the side so they wouldn't think he was holding hidden arms and get nervous. Bixby wanted him alive, he was sure of it. But one of them could get jumpy.

When he got to the dead bikers he quit breathing until he'd walked past the carnage. They had been hit with what amounted to heavy elk loads and the hot sun on the tissue damage had had considerable effect. More so, in a way, than the Sharps, because the copper-jacketed rounds had been made to mushroom in a more efficient way. Technology in action.

It took him some time to walk the meadow. He tried to count the paces so that he would know how far Carl would have to shoot but he lost count at three hundred. It had to be a good five hundred yards from Carl to the choppers. Halfway across, his arms became tired and he lowered them to his sides, half expecting a round but there was nothing, just the sound of the chopper engine getting louder as he came up to the drive.

He noted with satisfaction that his initial rounds into the truck had been accurate. The driver was dead, dead and distorted over against the door of the truck. There were two more bodies in the rear of the truck—he thought he'd only taken one in the back—and the panels were covered with holes. Some of them his; some from Carl.

The engine compartment on the first helicopter was likewise riddled, and there was the smell of hot fuel that had leaked out. They'd cut a line when they fired at it. He hoped the women weren't hurt.

"*John Smith stop there.*"

The public address was associated with the rear truck, the pickup, and they stopped him when he was still forty yards out.

"*Where is Carl Jackson?*"

John pointed back to the trees. "Dead," he yelled across the distance. "You killed him."

He heard a scream, knew it was Bev down in the ditch. Well. Nothing for it. Maybe her screaming would help them believe it.

"*Take off your clothes.*"

John nodded. They were pros, vets like himself, probably. There was always work for a vet, he thought. You could always find work. When you took a prisoner you made him strip—first rule of Nam. *If* you took a prisoner you made him strip. Put him at a psychological disadvantage. Reveal hidden weapons.

He took off his clothes, left his shorts on and was not surprised when the speaker boomed again.

"*Take off all your clothes.*"

He stripped naked. And knowing what they had in mind didn't help—he still felt inferior. He worked hard to overcome the feeling. Had only one thing now, only to get Bixby up out of the ditch so he could be hit. Just that one thing.

"*Come forward slowly.*"

John took a few steps forward, cut the distance to twenty-five yards, then stopped. "The women," he yelled. "Let the women go!"

There was silence out of the ditch in back of the trucks. He still could not see any people, but knew where they were from the microphone wire that ran down into the ditch from the cab of the truck.

"*Come forward!*"

"Let the women go!" John stood, naked in the field, and realized how ridiculous he must seem—a nude man in the Montana sun making demands from somebody he couldn't see, demands they had no reason whatsoever to honor. They could blow him away instantly if they wanted to—wipe him off the face of the earth like dust. Except that Bixby wanted him alive. They could not let the women go—John knew that. They could appear to do so, but they couldn't really let anybody go. Everybody had to die and the whole mess had to be cleaned up, or even Bixby's computers wouldn't be able to cover it all up. The police would have to react then. Armed assaults, bodies, helicopters, firefights—it couldn't be covered. Not this time. Everybody had to die.

But it was in character for John to try to get the women released. It was something Bixby would expect, and he wanted Bixby to be completely comfortable about everything he did; relaxed and confident.

The sun was hot and he realized suddenly how seldom a man's genitals are exposed to the heat of the sun. It was not uncomfortable, but he knew the sun would burn.... Bixby wouldn't let the women go. But he might fake doing it just to relax John.

Their heads appeared over the ditch. Both of them—Barbara and Bev. First the hair, then their faces. Bev with tears running down. Both of them riveted with fear; torn and pinned and their eyes tight with it as they walked towards him.

"Go past me," he said. "Go across the meadow. Go now. Go."

Bev walked jerkily, as she cried. Barbara reached a hand out to him but let it fall when he shook his head. "*Go*—go past me now. Out across the meadow. Run."

They started to trot, but Barbara fell because she was looking back at him. She got up and stopped. "He's going to kill you."

"I know. Go. Now. Run."

She held still for a moment. Then she nodded and started after Bev. John turned back to the trucks and helicopters and ditch. He moved forward to the edge of the ditch and looked down.

Two men wounded, huddled for cover against the near slope. Five other men, three of them armed with M-16's, two with handguns—the latter being the pilots of the two helicopters. Sitting against the far slope was a sixth man, rather thin but wiry, with dyed black hair and a mustache. He appeared to be about fifty. He was wearing a grey leisure suit and looked incongruously dapper in the dirt of the ditch and under the sweating hot sun. He was sitting upright, with his elbows on his knees, gazing down at the other men with an indifferent expression on his face, as if thinking of something totally unrelated to what was currently happening. When John stopped at the edge and looked down, he looked up.

"Bixby," John said.

The man stared up at him, as he stood naked on the rim, for a long moment, then nodded. "You've caused me some trouble." He said it as if he might be discussing a minor illness. "Mind telling me why?"

"Does it matter?"

"No. Not really. All I really want from you is the new code and an explanation of what you've done to my system. I don't need it. I want it. I can get along without it, do you understand?"

John looked down silently. It was a lie—Bixby needed the code or he wouldn't be here. But there wasn't anything he could say to it.

"I want it now."

"I forgot it."

Bixby turned to the man nearest him holding an M-16. "Shoot him in the leg, Earl."

There was an immediate explosion, the high flat keen of the M-16, and John's right leg went out from under him as he fell in the dirt. There was no pain, but when he looked down at his leg he saw a massive wound pouring blood and torn meat from his right thigh. He grabbed at it to stop the bleeding, grabbed at it because he knew the pain would come soon and he wouldn't be able to do anything then but scream.

"Does that help you remember?" Bixby had risen, was standing. The top of his head was over the top edge of the ditch but that still wasn't enough. There had to be more of him—his whole top half at least—for Carl to get the round off.

Somebody was making short hoarse bursts of sound and John realized with a start they were guttural rasps coming from his own throat. The pain had started, was nearly unbearable. He fought down his urges to scream, piled them in a corner of his brain. He had to get Bixby up higher. Had to stay in control of his mind and body long enough to get Bixby up next to him. He whispered a number. Any number but it had to come out in a whisper.

"What?" Bixby looked at him, moved across the ditch to hear him better. John lay slightly away from the edge of the ditch and Bixby had to climb up a bit to get closer.

But it still wasn't enough. Had to get him higher. Another whisper, another number but it wasn't the same as the first and it didn't matter anymore because the pain was working up from his leg now, a wild hot thing that took his brain and soul and made the screams come quicker so that he couldn't find the end of one or the beginning of another. He felt just flashes of red pain now, that gutted everything he was or ever had been; pain that took his eyes and mouth and drove his mind down into nothing, drove it like an arrow into a cave.

The last thing he saw, or thought he saw, was Bixby's head coming up higher and then suddenly jerk away in a red spray, but he couldn't be sure if it was real or something he dreamed.

Then he saw nothing.

TWENTY-TWO

It was an electric wheelchair, the kind that ran off a battery in the base and could be recharged at night while the patient slept. It was, as the hospital care had been, extremely expensive, but John didn't mind because the bank in Denver, actually a series of banks in Denver and several other western cities was picking up the entire tab. The banks were also paying him a substantial reward and a handsome on-going "consultation" fee—in truth, a fee to keep quiet about the enormously destructive inroads Bixby's operation had made into the banking system. The extent of the banks' gratitude had been very surprising to John, until he found out that Carl had done the negotiating with them while he was still in the hospital.

He remembered nothing until he came swimming up through the sick depths into a white room with bright lights and puked into a pan held by a middle-aged nurse. He'd then passed out again and was down that time until another rise into white lights and another puke with the same woman holding the pan.

Then pain. And drugs. And more pain and more drugs, with visions, seemingly hallucinations, of Barbara and Carl and Bev sitting in the room staring at him. The visions went together to make an indistinguishable blur until finally, at last, he could control the pain without the drugs and the flesh began to knit and heal. Two weeks. Three. It could have been years. At last, he opened his eyes to see Carl and Barbara, real people, sitting at a table on the other side of the white room.

"Hello," he'd said. "What day is it?"

Carl came over to the bed followed closely by Barbara. "Tuesday. How do you feel?"

"Drunk." He'd closed his eyes and opened them slowly. "Coming off a drunk. Did they take my leg?"

"No." Barbara stepped forward and tried to smile. "You'll be in a wheel chair for a while but they said you'll be able to walk."

"Water." His mouth felt full of dry old rags. Barbara reached over to the stand and held a glass with a straw for him while he drank. When he'd finished, he lay back and closed his eyes.

"Where's Bev?"

"She all right," Carl answered. "She's home taking care of the spread—she wanted to be here but somebody had to run it all."

"You got Bixby?"

"Clean. And two others when they came up out of the ditch to run. It was like ducks." Carl smiled grimly. "You were right. They started to split when they saw Bixby go down. One of them stopped to finish you but I took him first. Then drove like hell to save you."

"Thanks."

"Right. Listen, I know you aren't ready for

feeling it all around him, listening to the coyotes sing, yet having to sip Scotch in an effort to calm himself. the fact was that on those nights he saw nothing but his own obscurely busy thoughts.

One night, sitting on the porch like that and still not knowing for certain what was bothering him, his fingers seemed to find the buttons on the chair of their own accord, and he found himself moving silently, except for the subdued hum of the wheelchair motor, back into the house. He rolled down the ramp into Carl's office, then glided along until he sat facing the data terminal console. He felt quietly alone in the middle of the night.

After taking another sip of Scotch he propped the bottle between his legs, turned the keyboard on and opened the data line out through the phone system. Before he understood just what he was doing he was inside the Denver Data Center memory system.

Still without a clear idea as to why he was doing this, but feeling driven to it, John punched in the code he'd used to store and erase the information coming from Bixby's Los Angeles system—a code he'd revealed to nobody, just as he'd revealed to the investigators nothing about how big Bixby's network really was nor what he had done to all of it. He had withheld the code from the local banks, had not even mentioned to them that he had a private code, giving himself the excuse that he had to protect the money he had transferred into Carl's business account in Montana. But it was more than that. His deep reason for holding the code back was something else that he didn't understand. It was a whole world of something he didn't understand. . . .

That's it, he thought, looking at the glowing screen. There were no other lights on in the house; everybody else was asleep. That is exactly it. The whole world. The system could take over the whole world. It was all still there, all dormant and waiting except for Bixby's main crime computer. That was gone. But all the rest of the network's data he had been able to pump through Denver. There remained a whole data control system intricately interwoven into the world's economy—all of it just waiting for a new master.

For a new control.

He punched in the command to bring up any data that hadn't been sent to Denver and erased yet, but there was nothing. It was all cleaned out. Still, his private code was the last code to have controlled the entire system. It would be possible to work back through and re-energize the network from what he remembered as he'd worked to erase it. Only he knew about it—he and the data operators around the world who were now vulnerable to his command.

They're waiting for me, he thought. I could do this now. I could become immensely rich and powerful. Inside two years I could run the world's economy.

I could be the new control.

He took another long pull from the bottle and stared at the screen. His fingers began to work. He punched in the command that would put him back to the Boston computer—the only one in the crime network whose call letters he could remember at the moment—and found it true that his code was still operative, as he'd thought.

The Boston computer waited for him, like a blank check waiting to be signed. All its data were gone but its links to banks were still viable. It was just sitting there waiting for him to give the word—to raid accounts, to re-energize its entire network without the need for the defunct L.A. computer.

John's fingers hung over the keyboard as his mind grew rapt in contemplation. After Boston, what then?

Suddenly, footsteps sounded behind him. He spun his chair around.

"I got tired of sleeping alone," Barbara said. She came into the room and walked to his side. "I rolled over and you weren't there." She put a hand on his shoulder. "Don't you ever get sick of this stuff? What are you doing?"

John swallowed, looking at her. Behind were figures on a screen that meant nothing to her. All he had to do was type in the command and he would be the one; all of it would be his.

Her hand was warm and soft. Close on his shoulder, alive and as if part of him, he could feel it rubbing into his shoulder blades and into the soft edges of his mind as well. He understood what the hand could mean to him—a life, with Barbara, that had some human affection in it, perhaps even love, whatever love turned out to require of him, whatever it turned out to be. But it would be a life he could live; he was sure of that.

Whereas all the figures on the screen told him was that he could have money and power—power he knew damn well in his heart he would misuse again and again. He was not the man to take on that power. Nobody was.

He turned his chair and typed:

TERMINATE PROGRAM.

Then he shut the system down.

When he turned to face Barbara again, he had a grin on his face. "I wasn't doing much of anything. Right now I am sick of this stuff. Let's go to bed," he said.

More Best-selling Espionage and Suspense from Pinnacle Books

- [ ] **41-542-7 THE DUVEEN LETTER** $2.25
  by Edwin Leather
  Art detective Rupert Conway uncovers a skillful forgery that masks a KGB conspiracy and a link back to the depths of Nazi-occupied Europe.

- [ ] **41-442-0 THE MOZART SCORE** $2.25
  by Edwin Leather
  Rupert Conway acquires some rare Mozart scores: Are they valuable treasures or the key to the ultimate nuclear weapon?

- [ ] **41-432-3 THE PARIS DROP** $2.25
  by Alan Furst
  Double agents, assassins, wheeler-dealers, and femmes fatales in the City of Light.

- [ ] **41-443-9 THE VIENNA ELEPHANT** $2.50
  by Edwin Leather
  Soldier-art detective Rupert Conway solves murders, breaks spy rings, and hunts down stolen art treasures.

- [ ] **41-456-0 YOUR DAY IN THE BARREL** $1.95
  by Alan Furst
  The hero of The Paris Drop on a deadly chase through the streets of New York.

Buy them at your local bookstore or use this handy coupon
Clip and mail this page with your order

PINNACLE BOOKS, INC. – Reader Service Dept.
1430 Broadway, New York, N.Y. 10018

Please send me the book(s) I have checked above. I am enclosing $_____ (please add 75¢ to cover postage and handling). Send check or money order only—no cash or C.O.D.'s.

Mr./Mrs./Miss_____

Address_____

City_____ State/Zip_____

Please allow six weeks for delivery. Prices subject to change without notice.

GET ACQUAINTED!
THREE BESTSELLING ACTION/ADVENTURE SERIES FROM PINNACLE BOOKS

THE DESTROYER by Warren Murphy
Over 20 million copies sold to date!

☐ 41-216-9	Created, The Destroyer #1	$1.95
☐ 41-217-7	Death Check #2	$1.95
☐ 41-218-5	Chinese Puzzle #3	$1.95
☐ 41-219-3	Mafia Fix #4	$1.95
☐ 41-220-9	Dr. Quake #5	$1.95

THE EXECUTIONER by Don Pendleton
Over 25 million copies sold to date!

☐ 41-065-4	War Against The Mafia #1	$2.25
☐ 41-714-4	Death Squad #2	$2.25
☐ 41-699-7	Battle Mask #3	$2.25
☐ 41-068-9	Miami Massacre #4	$1.95
☐ 41-069-7	Continental Contract #5	$1.95

THE DEATH MERCHANT
by Joseph Rosenberger
Over 5.5 million copies sold to date!

☐ 41-345-9	Death Merchant #1	$1.95
☐ 41-346-7	Operation Overkill #2	$1.95
☐ 41-347-5	Psychotron Plot #3	$1.95
☐ 41-348-3	Chinese Conspiracy #4	$1.95
☐ 41-349-1	Satan Strike #5	$1.95

Canadian orders must be paid with U.S. Bank check or U.S. Postal money order only.

Buy them at your local bookstore or use this handy coupon

Clip and mail this page with your order

PINNACLE BOOKS, INC.—Reader Service Dept.
1430 Broadway, New York, NY 10018

Please send me the book(s) I have checked above. I am enclosing $_____ (please add 75¢ to cover postage and handling). Send check or money order only—no cash or C.O.D.'s.

Mr./Mrs./Miss _____

Address _____

City _____ State/Zip _____

Please allow six weeks for delivery. Prices subject to change without notice.